ANNIE'S ATTIC MYSTERIES

The Photo Album

Marlene Chase

AnniesMysteries.com

Published in Association with
Stenhouse & Associates, Ridgefield, Connecticut

Jacket & Book Design by
Lookout Design, Inc., Minneapolis, Minnesota

Library of Congress-in-Publication Data
Lady in the Attic / by Tara Randel
p. cm.
ISBN: 978-1-59635-305-3
I. Title
                    2009911072

10 11 12 13 14 | Printed in China | 10 9 8 7 6 5 4 3 2 1

AnniesMysteries.com
800-282-6643

~ PROLOGUE ~

When you are young and your heart is full of love, the world is a golden place. Every star whispers your name. In one shining moment, you are ageless, invincible.

The teenagers climbing the rocky ascent to the lighthouse know this inscrutable rising. A girl with fine gold hair blowing in the wind and eyes the color of the ocean holds the hand of the boy who brought her to life in the summer of her first love. Never in her sixteen years has she felt so alive, so on fire.

The boy has been in trouble now and then, but she can forgive him because he is different, terribly misunderstood, and no one cares for him. He has no one to mother him, and his father seldom knows if his son comes home or not. She takes a shuddering breath. No one will ever love Cagney as she does—as she always will.

They have sneaked out together on more than one occasion, but tonight will be special. They will leave this cramped little town where she came to spend the summer. Her mother will likely never forgive her. Summer in Maine had been a convenient solution, freeing her mother to take that business trip to London, the lucrative opportunity that will earn her the prestige she craves. The girl shivers, feels the familiar pain of wondering if her mother cares. . .really cares. . .about her.

Cagney cares. She knows it in the deepest part of her. She knows, too, that they will have to run away to be together. Auntie Beth would never agree to their marriage, and her mother? She shudders at the thought.

She had expected a dull summer, staying with her Auntie Beth in Stony Point, accompanying her to quilting bees or taffy pulls or whatever ladies do to pass their time. Instead, she met Cagney, who wanted to be called "Cage." She prefers the drama of his given name. But she admits to herself that he has captured her, that she will gladly follow him anywhere in this world or the next.

He is every girl's dream with dark sultry eyes in which sadness and mischief shine beneath unruly black hair. He is strong, brown as the wind-blown summer, and when he touches her, the world flames with beauty, and she is its queen. They will fly somewhere big enough to contain their burning hearts.

"Come on," he prods, pulling her up the hill to the point where the old lighthouse pierces the black sky. The night is cloudless, the bay boils with white water; immense combers charge up the pebbled beach. Beyond it the surf thunders and crashes against the rocks. They make their way higher. A flourishing stand of pines fringed with moonlight rises on one side.

The tiny ruined bungalow attached to the lighthouse has been left to the ospreys and the vagabond wind, but it has become their haven. She follows. Her hand, no longer cold, is burning in his. So what if her aunt wakes and finds her gone? So what if her mother abandons her when she finds out she has married this beautiful boy? Even if the whole world explodes, she will be with him, and they will never part.

They pause on the rocky landing, and the boy draws something from his pocket. Its crimson facets, struck by moonlight, gleam in oneness with the girl's shining eyes. She holds her hair back with shaking hands; he clasps the necklace around her slender white neck.

"I took it from his hiding place; he has lots more. . .but he'd kill me if he knew." He whispers the words bitterly, his eyes narrowing. The girl knows he speaks of that ghostly figure she's heard about but never seen—that one who makes Cagney do things boys shouldn't, who sparks her lover's beautiful eyes now with pain and cold fear.

"Oh, Cagney, I couldn't! You mustn't. . ."

"Cage. It's Cage," he says irritably and then softens his words with a smile that makes the fringe on his upper lip quiver. Once more he pulls her toward the bungalow. "Come on."

Suddenly he halts; she feels him go rigid beside her. "Oh, no! He's here. Go back. Go back!" he whispers fiercely, pressing her toward the dark row of trees. They see the boat perched crookedly on the rocks below the light, a sack outlined in the prow. They freeze and stare at the bungalow and the man coming out of it lurching toward them. Cagney pushes her back roughly with a hand gone clammy and cold. "Go!" he says fiercely.

And she runs. She runs to the trees, crouches there, her heart hammering in her thin chest. She is certain it can be heard over the roar of the surf. Her stomach lurches as she sees the man grab the boy, punch him hard in the stomach, double him over. Cagney fights back, but the man is strong. He yanks her lover up, knocks him down again on the rocky surface.

Something silvery flashes in the blackness. Is it a gun? She gasps and the world sways. She trembles with cold and fright and feels herself growing faint. She hears no sound. . . except the waves crashing against rock.

A figure moves to the edge of the cliff. He holds out arms over the water as though in sacrifice to some angry god. He releases something into the swirling waters. It rolls neatly into the watery crypt below where the surf crashes brazenly over the rock. "Where is Cagney?" She feels the world falling away. She can't look!

When she peers through her trembling fingers, she does not see Cagney. A man stands alone, his face white and hard in the glow of moonlight. He searches the surrounding landscape and the stand of trees where she hides.

She wants to run to Cagney; somewhere he's hurt and alone. All alone! But the man Cagney feared is looking straight at her through disembodied eyes that gleam nearly yellow in the darkness. Those eyes that will linger in her nightmares; she will never forget them.

She smothers her terrified cries and zigzags through the woods. The beautiful scarlet necklace, her wedding gift, burns against her throat.

Her aunt's eyes fill with tears as she hears the story. A deadly silence ensues, broken only by the girl's sobbing and the relentless ticking of the kitchen clock. Then she is whisked away from Stony Point, taken back to New York that very night to her mother, who has just returned from England.

The wounded child, not yet a woman, will keep her silence about the terror of that night. The stars will no longer whisper her name; the ocean will roll mindlessly on, but her summer love is engraved on her heart for all time. Years later when the summer people and the townies remember the boy who disappeared, she will keep him alive in her heart.

No one else will ever know that she was at the lighthouse that night; that Cagney is gone—perhaps forever—and that someone else has been there, too. Someone with odd amber eyes furrowed by thick dark brows. Those eyes are etched in her consciousness forever like the very visage of evil.

*I, Elizabeth Holden, being of sound mind, do hereby bequeath
the whole of my estate with all its contents to my beloved
granddaughter Annie Holden Dawson, which estate, located
at Number 1, Ocean Drive, Stony Point, Maine, shall become
her property solely upon my death.*

So it was that Annie had come to Grey Gables, the two-story Victorian house that had called her back from
another life, from another age. Grey Gables, purchased by
her grandparents after World War II, had been her summer
haven during childhood. Her grandmother had been her port
in the storm, her North Star. She couldn't just turn Gram's
home over to strangers, sell it off like an ugly stepsister.

"Stony Point is spectacular," she told LeeAnn, imagining her petite blond daughter sipping a cup of hazelnut coffee, cell phone to her ear. In the background she heard the
high voices of the twins, John and Joanna.

Brookfield, Texas, was a long way from Stony Point.
It was like another continent, she thought. She surveyed the
majestic New England vista from Grey Gables' wide front
porch. Beyond the lawn, she could see the ocean shimmering in the great blue cradle of sky.

That ocean had witnessed the generations come and
go. It held many a story and bore the burdens of mankind

over the centuries, never breaking a cadence. Sometimes its melodies and rhythms were gentle; other times they crashed with thundering power. What secrets it might tell if it were given to speech, rather than music. What might it say about her, about those long-ago days when she was very young?

"I watched the sun rise over the ocean this morning," she said, breaking her own reverie. "It was like a great roly-poly creature climbing out of the water and shaking itself all over."

"Still a morning person, even when you don't have to be," LeeAnn said. "It sounds wonderful, Mom, but I thought you'd be ready to come home by now."

"I'm still going through Gram's things. I don't think she ever threw anything away. And frankly, I'm finding it hard to decide what to do with it all. There's so much that reminds me of her and of the summers I spent here. And Grey Gables needs some TLC too, that's for sure."

She paused, her gaze arrested by distant white sails on water so still it might have been glass or a giant mirror. "Grey Gables is just like I remembered it. Perhaps a bit more weathered, but so regal, so very like Gram. The attic is a virtual treasure trove. There's so much here, so much living, so much love." A lump sprang to her throat. "I just need time to sort it all out."

She said good-bye to her daughter and sat mesmerized by the tranquil scene before her. It was quite changed from yesterday's raging gray-green panorama. Boots appeared around the corner of the porch and sat down to clean her sleek gray coat and white paws. "Aren't you the persnickety one, Miss Boots?" she said warmly. The eccentric feline had belonged to Gram. "That's the only reason I put up with you." Boots paused in her ritual to give Annie her most officious stare. "I know, I know," Annie said. "You were here first."

Alice MacFarlane had brought Boots to Annie on that first day she'd arrived at Grey Gables. "She was Betsy's," said Alice. "I'm just returning her to Grey Gables."

When her girlhood friend had turned up on Annie's doorstep, cat in arms, the years had melted away as they renewed a friendship begun decades earlier.

Where had all the years gone? Annie wondered. She recalled how she had loved it here as a child. She savored those long-ago summers filled with homemade pastries and ice cream, picnics and parades and sitting on the broad front porch until the night was too old for fireflies but never too old for stars. Yes, someday soon she would bring LeeAnn and Herb here. She must never let the distance separate them as she had allowed it to separate her and her grandmother during recent years.

The tyranny of the urgent, she thought. It could rob you of the truly important. If she'd learned nothing else she'd learned that. "Love does not end as all else must, does not surrender to the storm or to the dust." The words of the poet celebrated love's tenacity, the wonder of it.

How blessed she had been to be raised by loving parents who encouraged her to follow her dreams. After college she'd met Wayne, the love of her life. God had given them LeeAnn and the chance to work together operating their car dealership in Brookfield, Texas. She'd loved the Lone Star state, the big, big heart of it and its people. But none was as good or generous as her beloved Wayne. Could it be possible that two years had passed since his massive heart attack?

I've had a heart attack of my own, she whispered without words. And just when she knew nothing could save her from her sudden melancholy, Boots leaped upon her lap, startling her and rolling herself into a furry ball. Annie stroked the soft gray head. Well, for better or worse, she and Boots had each other, and Boots had an intuitive sense for knowing when she was needed.

Annie shivered a little, not so much from the coolness of the Maine morning as from a pang of loneliness. Home was so far away. She sighed and watched the steam rise from the porcelain cup on the wicker table. She'd figured settling Gram's estate might take a few weeks, perhaps a month or two, and then she'd go back to Texas. It was her home, after all, but Stony Point was taking on a life of its own. Forgotten treasures had been uncovered and new friendships forged that were becoming surprisingly important to her.

She breathed deeply and looked out to the garden in the side yard. It had been overgrown and weedy, but she and her handyman, Wally Carson, had been working on that. The perennials had taken firm hold—Michaelmas daisies and phlox from white to flaming crimson. Calendulas and clematis struggled among the persistent weeds. A garden, she thought, is always a series of losses set against a few triumphs. Perhaps like life itself.

Grey Gables had seen its triumphs and defeats as well. It was hers now to do with as she thought best, though it was less hers than Gram's. Perhaps it never would be more.

She'd enjoyed leisurely walks along Stony Point's coast, all the way to the graceful little platinum beach set in a circular cove. At the eastern tip, Butler's Lighthouse stood like a grand dame watching over the children who came summer after summer to play at her feet. The summer people were arriving again. Soon the water would be teeming with them. It would welcome them as it had welcomed her so many years before.

She put Boots down gently. Another cup of coffee might just give her enough energy to explore the boxes she had brought down from the attic and to wreak a little vengeance on the weeds.

"Good morning, Annie!" Alice MacFarlane called, her soprano voice as vibrant as her blue eyes. She ascended the walk with quick steps, her sandals slapping the stones and her white blouse flapping over her skinny blue jeans. "Have bread, will share!" she quipped, holding out a foil-wrapped loaf. "It's a new recipe I'm serving my Princessa Jewelry party tonight."

"And I'm to be the guinea pig?" Annie asked with mock concern.

"Ayuh, as we Mainers say."

"Well, I'm ready, willing, and hungry. I was just going to get another cup of coffee. Now I'll get two."

Annie returned with coffee, knife, and Gram's Aster Blue plates. Alice cut the fragrant lemony bread, her slender fingers moving deftly. Alice liked to wear a ring on every finger, even the thumb. It was one way to display her wares. In addition to selling jewelry, she held Divine Décor parties and could cross-stitch with amazing speed.

"This is heavenly," Annie said. "Thanks for choosing me as tester."

Alice leaned back in the wicker chair and heaved a great sigh. "And *this* is heavenly," she breathed, extending her arms to encompass the view from the porch. "This view is magnificent. It's been part of my life forever, but I never tire of looking at it."

Annie nodded, glad for Alice's exuberant company, for the friend who'd known her as a child. It was great that they had this chance to get to know each other—really know each other—as women.

"Do you remember how we used to climb to the top of Butler's Lighthouse and pretend we were damsels in distress?" Alice shook her auburn hair back and struck an elaborate pose. "Help me! Help me!"

"Then we'd burst out laughing until we couldn't breathe," Annie finished.

Alice clasped her hands behind her head. "Those were great old days. Why do we have to grow up?"

It was just a nostalgic observation, but Annie knew something of the heartache behind it. Alice gave everyone the impression that she walked on air, that the world was a lark, but it hadn't been easy for her. Alice and John MacFarlane had divorced after a decade of disappointment. John, a dashing land developer, had great dreams and a wandering eye.

"I guess growing up isn't so bad if we keep our dreams alive," Annie said.

"And learn from our mistakes," Alice added.

"Well, this bread is certainly no mistake. Your Princessa clients are going to love it and buy a thousand rings and bracelets!" Annie reached for her paisley crochet tote bag; she loved working outside on Gram's old porch. As a child, she'd been fascinated with Gram's beautiful cross-stitched canvases.

Since Wayne had gone, she'd found herself more and more drawn to the joy of creating something beautiful and functional. She'd started with knitting but later experimented with the crochet hook. For a beginner, it was less frustrating. If one stitch broke, stitches above and below remained intact. Because of the complex looping, the stitches on either side were not as likely to come loose unless put under a lot of stress. She'd made scarves and mittens and graduated to more challenging items such as the sweater she was making for Joanna. Often Alice brought her cross-stitch over and the two would work together.

"I'm so glad you decided to come back to Stony Point." Alice leaned forward in the chair. "You are going to stay, aren't you?" She cocked her head in an endearing way. "Please?"

"I don't know, Alice. I'm not ready to leave yet, though. There's so much work to be done on this old place, and Gram was a terrible pack rat, you know."

"Your grandmother saved a lot of things, including my sanity!" Alice shrugged a little and looked off toward the garden. "When I was going through the divorce, she was my saving grace."

"She was one great lady," Annie said, missing Gram anew. "She saved a lot of things that had special meaning to her. I guess that's why I want to take my time sorting through them. I think she'd want that."

"You're a lot like her. In fact, I think you favor her." Alice looked into Annie's face with a studious frown. "Yes, the shape of the nose, that Scandinavian coloring. . ."

"The wrinkles, the gray hairs. . ." Annie added.

Alice reached over and gave her arm a shove. "Not!" she exclaimed. "Don't you know half of Stony Point's females look at you with envy?"

"Right. And there's this bridge in Brooklyn. . ." Annie put the sweater she was crocheting down on a small trunk that was part of the wicker porch ensemble and picked up an album with a faded maroon cover. "Speaking of the old days, Boots and I found this when I was going through some things up in the attic. It's full of pictures from when we were kids."

Alice pulled her chair closer and leaned in eagerly. "Oh, that's so cool," she said. "Look, there we are with our pails. And you had just found that speckled conch. You've got it held up to your ear like a telephone."

"And you were smeared with so much sand no one would know you if it weren't for that mop of hair that always got redder in summer," Annie said.

"You were older, Miss Bookworm. I think you tolerated me because I was always a captive audience when you were reading."

"When you're kids, a few years can be a lot, but the gap shortens when you're grown up," Annie said wistfully.

"But I'm going to remind you every chance I get that

I'm the younger woman. Whereas you. . ."

"Never mind," Annie interrupted laughing. "We did have fun, though."

"That's odd," Annie said.

"What?"

"Look at that boy there—the one close to the edge of the pier. The dark one with black hair blowing in the wind." Annie pointed to a youth, maybe fifteen or sixteen years old. He was slight, almost delicate. A stripe lay across his neck and shoulder where a fence post had cast a long shadow. "And he's in other pictures too." She flipped back another page. "There, see. He's by the lobster shack just looking out to sea like some miniature mariner. There's something so solitary about him."

"Hmm," Alice murmured, a perplexed frown on her forehead. "It could be anyone. Gosh, he's so young." Alice leaned in closer, screwed up her slender nose. Could even be Ian Butler," she said with a cocky smile. "Maybe even way back then he was planning what he'd do when he became mayor."

Annie had grown fond of Ian Butler, a widower whose long-established family ran the local sawmill. As mayor he was thoroughly immersed in the activities of the town. Something strong and proud in him answered to the pioneer spirit in her, and they'd become friends.

Single ladies in town, including Alice, found Ian attractive. She poked her friend's shapely shoulder. "Of course it's not Ian. This boy doesn't look anything like him. So who do you suppose it might be? If you can get your mind off the town's most eligible bachelor. . .

"Summer people," Alice confirmed. "We didn't know many of them."

"You knew me."

"That's because we practically lived next door. Besides," Alice assumed a serious pose, "with us it was fate."

"Destiny, to be sure," Annie agreed, laughing. "But are you sure you don't know who this boy is? There's something so. . .I don't know. . .tragic about him. Look at those eyes. They're so. . .as though no light shines in them. And he's not smiling in any of these shots. Look close. What do you see in those eyes?"

"Nothing, but I can see something in those green eyes of yours, Annie Dawson. You've gotten the bug again. The sleuthing germ. And we all caught it from you over your last attic discovery. We hadn't had so much fun in years." She clapped her hands together. "Bring the album on Tuesday. When the girls get their heads together, there's no limit to the mischief we can get into." Alice jumped up. "Well, I'm going to be late if I don't get back."

Annie waved Alice off and watched her trip lightly down the stairs, her hair billowing like a cloud behind her. Sunlight glanced off her bejeweled fingers. It was something of a miracle, Annie thought, finding Alice again after all these years. Perhaps it wasn't fate or even destiny but a gift to be opened and shared. Maybe with a lonely young person like the one in the photo.

She turned back to see Boots sitting on the album, her tail wagging slowly across the shirtless boy's chest. Who was he? What had been his destiny? Oh, Gram, what

have you done? You and all those intriguing treasures in
the attic.

~ 2 ~

Annie turned off the mostly grim television news, eager to meet the new day. Every moment was a gift, after all, wasn't it? That philosophy was ingrained like an old habit or maybe a dominant gene from another generation. It had been Gram's way. Annie liked that it had become hers too. And today was Tuesday—a day she looked forward to. The Hook and Needle ladies had become her friends, helping her get acquainted with her new surroundings. New, yet somehow so familiar.

She opened the front door to accommodate Boots, who waited there patiently but with an insistent expression on her whiskery face. Boots seldom meowed; such displays were unsophisticated, beneath her.

Annie paused in the wide entryway with its steps leading to the upstairs bedrooms and the attic. She had planned to quickly determine what to do with everything and put the house up for sale, but Grey Gables had a way of growing on a person. And the more repairs she did on the old place, the more endearing it became.

She scooped up a newspaper from the living room, a spacious but inviting room with a flowered sofa and a comfortable jade-green chair. Her grandmother's beautifully stitched pillows portrayed scenes from Stony Point: wildflowers on a windblown hill, a gray-slatted barn in autumn, a cottage by the ocean with sea oats bending in the wind and great craggy rocks full of character like old men.

The best piece of furniture in the room was a rococo accent table from the latter part of the eighteenth century. It featured a serpentine apron embellished with a fleur-de-lis pattern of swirling leaves. The table, with its single drawer, was placed prominently beneath a wide front window dressed only in a sheer valance to provide an unobstructed view of the ocean.

Across the entry hall in the dining room was a six-chair extension table of dark oak. Behind the hutch's patterned doors, Gram's favorite Aster Blue china gleamed. The dining room was elegant but seldom used. She preferred the large, warm kitchen in the back of the house next to the family room.

Memories of her childhood loomed everywhere. The Raggedy Ann and Andy dolls lay on the white chenille spread in one of the east bedrooms. And just yesterday she had found the little Russell Library of Games: Old Maid, Authors, Dr. Quack, Slap Jack, Animal Rummy, and Cross-Word. She and Gram had played them all; sitting outside on the wide front porch while they sipped a special brew of cherry lemonade that Gram served with thin lime slices.

The house held so much living, caring, and dreams. Its secrets were embedded in every corner. The doors of Grey Gables had opened wide for all who sought shelter, solace, love. A house should be like that: a light that beckoned and offered refuge.

She grabbed her crochet tote, which she'd left under the hall table, and stepped out on the porch. Passing the photo album on the wicker trunk, she tucked it inside her bag. Perhaps someone would recognize the mysterious boy in the snapshots.

Who was he? And why was he always off on his own? Last night she'd dreamed about him, a shadowy figure with no shirt who would pop up several yards ahead of her, an odd smile on his pathetic face. And just as she was about to catch up to him, he disappeared. Strange that a person could dream of someone she'd never known—well, didn't think she knew. He might be anyone. He could be someone on the other side of the world or a neighbor walking around Stony Point at this very moment.

She was about to step into her Malibu to make her way down Ocean Drive when she saw a man standing at the end of the block, looking intently at Grey Gables. Fashionable chinos and a silky blue shirt effectively showed off slim hips and well-developed biceps. A white cardigan or sweatshirt was slung over one shoulder.

She ducked into the car and waited, knowing she couldn't be seen from the street. The light-skinned stranger remained inert, classic head with short blond hair glowing reddish in the sun. It was too early in the season for a tan to take hold, but he'd definitely look good in one. His neck sported no camera, the perennial tourist giveaway. He had about him the aura of success; a look lethally attractive to women. She frowned, recognizing that she was enjoying this handsome improvement to the view.

Something about him evoked a sudden sense of loss. It had been so good to walk down the street with Wayne, to know that they looked good together and that people envied their obvious happiness. It must have been obvious because she had been positively swollen with it. She and Wayne would grow old together, become so much a part of each other that people might not be able to tell the difference between them.

She slapped herself mentally. What was wrong with her? Why was she staring at a perfect stranger? And he *was* perfect. But it was a bit unnerving to see him ogling Grey Gables. What was he looking at anyway? And why? She started the motor and gunned it hard down the long driveway. When she got to the road, he was moving on with a slow, sauntering gait, eyes straight ahead.

She switched on the radio. "Be sure to tune in this afternoon for All Things Considered," said the announcer, "brought to you by National Public Radio." She laughed. There were some things she was determined not to consider, and that included any romantic entanglement. Alice might be looking, but she definitely was not.

She drove toward the square and found it already alive with townies and summer people, though it was only ten o'clock in the morning. She'd left early to look up Wally Carson, the local handyman. The screens needed some serious attention, and she had hoped Wally might be able to restore Gram's gateleg table.

She turned away from the square and drove toward Grand Avenue where Wally often hung out after he dropped little Emily off at kindergarten and Peggy at the Cup and Saucer. A lifetime resident, Wally had been a troubled teen, redeemed from his ne'er-do-well proclivities by the vivacious Peggy. Six-year-old Emily had heightened his ambition to make something of himself. He doted on the child with touching tenacity. Annie had been happy to offer Wally the chance to ply his handyman skills at Grey Gables; there was plenty to keep him occupied there. She found him sitting languidly in the sun, his shirt oddly draped over his left shoulder.

"Wally?" As Annie drew near, she realized that his left arm hung in a fresh cast. "What have you done to yourself?"

He squinted up at her and struggled to rise. "Don't get up," she said, and dropped down beside him on the pier. Wally Carson liked to hang out with his buddies who were fishermen. She turned to him, waited, sensing his melancholy.

"Hello, Mrs. D." He nodded, a shock of unruly black hair creasing an eyebrow. "Did this falling out of a tree. Stupid, huh?"

"I'm so sorry, Wally. Does it hurt much?"

"Nah, but it's a bummer. A one-armed handyman ain't gonna be much use to you. I'm sorry." He looked out to sea, the tiny wrinkles around his eyes deepening.

It wasn't going to be easy for them without his income. Peggy didn't earn much as a waitress, even in summer when tips were better. "I'm really sorry, Wally. But you'll mend and be as good as new." She regretted the patronizing sound of her voice and sat with him on the sun-drenched dock. They watched the boats circle and drift around gaudily colored buoys. "I guess there are more lobsters caught in Maine than anywhere else in the country," she said.

"Yup. Delicious little devils, and they bring a good price too."

Fishermen were throwing some of the lobsters back

into the water. "What's the regulation size for harvesting?" she asked.

"Three and a quarter inches," he said, brightening. Wally loved to talk about fishing and especially lobstering. "You gotta measure them from the eye socket to the start of the tail. They weigh about a pound and a quarter, legal size."

"You know your lobsters," Annie said. "Tourists are sure fascinated by them," she added, seeing a group of them clustering around the shack at the far end of the pier. "It's a wonder there are any left in the ocean."

Annie could tell Wally was feeling better just talking about something he loved. She hoped one day he'd have his own boat and equipment. He was a good handyman, but he was no landlubber. She'd have a talk with Ian, whose brother did some lobstering. Even a one-armed guy could help set the traps and earn a little money on the side. And certainly, Wally and Peggy needed it.

"Well," she said, rising, "I'm off to A Stitch in Time."

"Yup. Peg had her stuff in the car when I dropped her off. You gals have fun."

"Remember, I've got several jobs waiting for you when that thing comes off." She pointed to the ungainly gauzy appendage and felt a pang in her own left arm. Wally was a bit of a rogue sometimes, but he had a good heart. She thought he wasn't unlike the boy in the photo album. Same disheveled black hair and troubled eyes. Wally was grown up, of course, and a little thicker through the middle. *Right, Annie Dawson,* she told herself. *You're seeing the mystery boy in every dark-complexioned kid in Stony Point. Do you really think it's going to be that easy to identify him?* Well, if so, maybe she'd no longer be bothered by the haunted eyes in the photos.

She drove back up Maple to Main Street, past the movie theater, and parked several doors away from the yarn store. Stony Point could be a busy place in summer when the tourists descended, but who minded? Every shop and business had spruced up. Flowers overflowed in urns and window boxes. Dress to Impress had a brand new sign and modern mannequins posing in the window.

She nearly collided with someone stepping out of the Cup and Saucer. "Oh, sorry, Ian. I was looking for. . .I guess I *wasn't* looking."

"Annie, it's nice to see you." Ian Butler grasped her hand firmly. Busy as he always seemed, he took time to greet a person properly. He looked directly at them, rather than beyond to the next task on his list. She liked that about him. Politicians, she supposed, had to learn that fine art, but she rather suspected it came naturally to Ian.

"Hi. I was hoping I'd run into you."

"You were?" he asked with a raised eyebrow and twinkle in his gray eyes.

"To ask you something," she added quickly, "about Wally."

Ian was on the low side of fifty, with carefully trimmed hair the color of good coffee. A little cream swirled at his temples. Arianna, Ian's wife, had been a stunning woman, a former actress. People said she fostered little theater productions. Visitors came from as far away as Kittery and Oregon County to take in a play. And of course there were the summer people eager to see a good show.

When Arianna died suddenly of a brain aneurysm, Ian had been shattered; Alice told her he'd taken a long sabbatical in upstate New York before throwing himself back into the life of Stony Point. Alice was of the opinion that his feverish enthusiasm constituted an escape from despair.

"Town's looking good, wouldn't you say?" he mused, gesturing toward the vibrant red petunias blossoming in the Cup and Saucer's window box. "The town's filling up. Every day I see new faces. What about Wally?" That was Ian. He had an agenda and he didn't waste words, but he wasn't without concern for Stony Point's citizens.

"You know, Wally's been doing some work for me at Grey Gables. But I learned this morning that he's going to be laid up for a while. He broke his arm trimming a tree."

Ian raised an eyebrow, dropped his hands into the pockets of his jeans. "Tough break," he said. He grinned ruefully. "Sorry."

She gave him a smile to acknowledge his joke and shook her head. "You can say that again. They barely get by as it is, and now there'll be only Peggy's salary. I was wondering if your brother Todd might be able to use Wally. His lobster business is growing. Maybe Wally could help set traps or clean the stalls from time to time. Even a one-armed person can hose down a dock. Wally really needs a job. . .with pay."

Ian looked at her with a quizzical smile. "Championing social causes now, are we? Don't tell me you've run out of curiosities in that attic?"

He was only teasing as he often did, but she wasn't going

to let him one-up her. "Oh, no," she said sweetly. "There are plenty of curiosities; I've even met a few on the streets of Stony Point."

"Aha," he said with a good-natured smile. He stuffed his hands into his pockets and jingled his coins and keys, always his signal that he had places to go, people to see. "I'll speak to Todd. Oh, and good luck with your curiosities." And he hurried across the street, waving to a passing motorist in a blue pickup.

Annie laughed as she clutched her needlework bag and pushed through the door of A Stitch in Time. If there was a way to help Wally and Peggy, she'd find no more willing ally than the large-hearted Ian Butler.

~ 3 ~

Annie stepped into A Stitch in Time, where the aroma of freshly brewed coffee rose in a welcoming wave. She put her tote bag down at her chosen chair in the circle of women. The room was perfect for their meetings: big enough to spread out their supplies and small enough to be cozy.

Across the room, Alice was chatting with sales associate Kate Stevens, who wore a denim jacket embossed with ladybugs and daisies. Most likely the jacket was her own design. Kate's dark hair curved around her face in a blunted page boy that was longer in front than in back—very stylish. She waved and flashed her bright smile.

"Hi, Alice," Annie called, moving their way and sitting down between them. "Morning, Kate."

"How are things coming at Grey Gables?" Kate asked. "It's such a charming place; I've always loved it. It's nice to see the garden gaining ground. I was passing last week, and I saw the flower beds. Your grandma would be pleased; she had a green thumb if ever there was one. What are those tall, spiky purple things?"

"That's blue salvia. With red geraniums and white phlox, it will be quite Fourth of July, don't you think?" Annie liked Kate. She had recently been through a divorce. After putting up with Harry's drinking for years, she had finally had enough. But she still loved Harry. "That jacket is gorgeous," Annie told her now. "It has your touch on it. Love those ladybugs."

Looking around, she caught Stella Brickson's eye. "Hello, Stella," she said. Stella returned a greeting and continued her conversation with Gwendolyn Palmer, wife of the local banker. Gwen waved and smiled. Then Peggy Carson arrived, wearing her pink uniform but whipping off her white apron. Her short dark hair, often jelled into creative positions, was brushed back from her forehead and held in place with a turquoise barrette. A waitress at the Cup and Saucer, Peggy always took an early lunch on Tuesdays so she could join the group. A beginning quilter, her first project was a Disney princess patchwork for her daughter Emily.

"Hi, everyone," she said somewhat shyly and lacking her usual vigor.

Annie put a hand on her shoulder. "I'm so sorry about Wally's arm. I saw him down by the pier and he told me what happened."

"Yes," Peggy said softly. "He was trimming a tree over at the Hodges place, and I don't know how he did it, but suddenly he was on the ground." She rolled her blue eyes, and Annie saw that there were tears in them. "I know I'm a baby, but it couldn't come at a worse time. We were going to enroll Emily in Myra's school of dance, but. . ." She broke off and began lifting her quilt blocks from a plastic bin.

Peggy was the youngest member of the needlework club. It was hard not to like the exuberant, large-hearted girl who had waited so long for a baby. She liked to wear intricately painted fingernails with pictures of Malibu sunsets, flamingos, or miniature daisies with purple centers. Good thing her sister was a beautician; on her salary Peggy could never afford them.

Annie longed to simply give Peggy the money for the lessons, but she knew that would embarrass her and Wally. Instead she fussed over and complimented the quilt blocks. Cinderella, Snow White, and Belle danced across green and pink squares, accompanied by Jasmine, Ariel, Pocahontas, and Mulan. Soon a complete Disney princess quilt would have to include Rapunzel and Tiana from "Princess and the Frog." Annie traced Cinderella's beautiful ball gown with her finger. "These are lovely; such wonderful colors. Emily is going to love this. Your embroidery on the gowns is beautiful!"

Peggy brightened, but her mind was still on Wally's accident and the financial squeeze it could bring. "Maybe it won't be so bad. Tips will be better now that the summer's coming."

"Wally was telling me about lobstering," Annie said.

"Someday he wants to have his own smack, or at least something besides that old peapod. Did he tell you that?"

You didn't have to hang around Maine very long before you learned that a "smack" was what some lobstermen called their boats. They were small sailing vessels with tanks inside and holes to allow sea water to circulate, keeping the lobsters fresh. A peapod was basically a canoe with a wide center and narrow ends. "No," she replied, "but you can tell the ocean is where Wally's heart is."

Just then Mary Beth, A Stitch in Time's owner, strode in.

"Sorry I'm late, girls. I had a little errand to run. I'm sure Kate welcomed you." She broke off, more flustered than Annie had ever seen her. Nor had she known her to be late before. Mary Beth ran a tight ship and didn't suffer fools gladly. A single woman with more guts per pound than most, she commanded respect. She had started her shop several decades ago and become so much a part of Stony Point that no one could imagine the place without her.

Annie watched with appreciation as Mary Beth made the rounds of the group, praising each one's particular project or offering a suggestion for a trouble spot. Everyone craved her approval and worked hard to earn it. When Mary Beth stepped off to the side to help a customer, Peggy leaned over and whispered in Annie's ear. "Did you hear what happened?"

Annie gave her a puzzled look.

"Well," Peggy continued, "she had to run home about 9:30 this morning to get something she needed, and when she got there someone had been in her house. Nothing at all was taken, but she was sure someone had been inside. Mary Beth is so particular, and one of her pictures had been moved on the mantel."

"What did she do?"

"Nothing. What could she do? But she was really upset."

Over a misplaced picture? Most likely she'd been dusting, moved it herself, and forgot, Annie thought. Well, little things were important to Mary Beth. Her cottage was spare and spotless, a true New Englander's dwelling.

Mary Beth had returned and was clearing her throat.

"I've been thinking that we need to do something really different. You're all getting quite professional. And not to brag, but I taught you well." She laughed at her own boast and quickly resumed her speech. "We've made quilts and hats and mittens for every worthy cause. Now I think we should do something on a larger scale, something special."

Mary Beth talked on in short, punchy sentences without dislodging a single iron-gray curl. She crossed her arms over her burgundy smock. "I'm thinking of a needlework fair. It will be a really grand event for the whole town and all the summer visitors. Everyone could display her very best projects, and we'll have a judging. . ."

A collective gasp arose from the members. They looked around at one another and back at Mary Beth.

"Well, why not?" she continued. "You're all good at what you do; it could be a real hit. We'll hold it near the end of summer before everyone leaves. We can sell materials from the shop and have concessions too. You know, sandwiches, sweets, coffee, soda, whatever we can get the good folks of Stony Point to contribute. We could also throw in a few antique pieces—donated, of course—and have an auction for a good cause."

"And the good cause?" Gwendolyn queried with a lift of her pale eyebrows. Her blond hair was drawn tightly back to reveal a pleasantly lined face. Pale blue-gray eyes sparkled with intelligence. A chic silk scarf draped her left shoulder. Social causes were Gwen's forte. She and John Palmer, known as pillars of the community, were always eager to foster the good image of Stony Point.

"Why, the Hook and Needle Club, but of course we'll

donate a part of the proceeds for the church food pantry. That way, Reverend Wallace will be eager to support the event."

"What about Ian? You know how particular he is about everything in town. What if he doesn't approve of a needlework fair?" Alice asked.

Mary Beth wrapped her arms more tightly across her chest. "Whatever's good for Stony Point will be okay with Ian."

Excited whispers gave way to a general hubbub as the idea took root and grew. Peggy was sure the Cup and Saucer would supply the coffee, and Alice was already starting one of her famous lists, without which Annie was sure she wouldn't remember to get up in the morning. Everyone was assigned to a committee.

Mary Beth turned to Annie. "Maybe you and Alice can handle the concessions." She gave Annie a meaningful look. "And if you could throw in a Betsy Original, it would positively be the icing on the cake."

"That's a marvelous idea," Stella spoke up. "Elizabeth's canvases are second to none."

Annie thought she saw a quick tear spring up before Stella looked away to resume her handwork. Annie was warmed by Mary Beth's trust in her and by Stella's high praise for her grandmother's work, Stella and Gram having been girlhood friends.

"I'll go through the attic and see what I can find. And speaking of the attic. . ." Annie drew the maroon-covered photo album from her crochet tote. "Alice and I were going through this old album, and we found the neatest pictures.

Some of you might even be in them."

There was a commotion as everyone rushed to see the pictures. Mary Beth looked at the album over Peggy's shoulder.

"That's you, Alice," Peggy said triumphantly. "I'd know that little snub nose and mop of red hair anyplace. Of course, I was but a speck in my mother's eye then," she added proudly.

Peggy wasn't likely to know anyone else in the photos, including the young boy in the background. So far, no one had even remarked about the shadowy figure in the photo that was some twenty years old. Annie was interested in Mary Beth's take. Though she'd likely been about forty then, she might have known the kids around town.

"Isn't that Ian?" Gwen pointed to a slim young man with a crew cut who was raising the American flag at the bandstand. He was wearing khakis and a red polo shirt, a look of solemn pride on his face.

"Why, I believe it is," chuckled Alice. "A Yankee Doodle Dandy." Appreciation was clearly visible in her mischievous blue eyes.

Annie honed in on her mission and pointed to the figure of the mystery boy at the rear of the summertime crowd. The face, thin and tanned, his tousled black hair obscuring one eye. "Who do you suppose he is?"

"Our Annie's been bitten by the mystery bug again," Alice chanted from across the room. And there was laughter and reminiscing about items Annie had found in the attic: a chamber pot with hieroglyphics that turned out to be Polish, World War II medals, a Pinkerton safe stuffed with buttons, a few of which had some value once they found a way to crack the thing open.

A general buzz took over as the women tried to identify the boy. A name was offered, mulled over, and then shot down by the others as they exchanged perplexed looks. Annie moved the album over to Mary Beth, who had perhaps been around the longest. She had loved poring over other objects brought to the meetings.

"Here he is in this picture. And here. . ." One after the other she pointed out snapshots that contained the image of the nameless boy. "He's always there. But not with anyone. He looks so sad, so isolated."

"What do you think, Mary Beth?" Kate asked her.

When no immediate answer came, Annie looked up from the album and across to Mary Beth. Had she been that pale before, while she outlined her plan for a needlework fair? Her coral lipstick seemed suddenly garish in her blanched face. But she'd been upset, Annie remembered, by whatever had happened at her house that morning.

As quickly as the pallor came, it disappeared. Mary Beth, leaning over Gwen's shoulder, peered into the album. She pursed her lips in studied concentration. "Well, he does look somewhat familiar. Likely summer people. Stony Point's had a lot of them over the years." She nodded. "We'll put our heads together and see what we can come up with. If anyone can discover who this mystery boy is, you girls can."

More excited chatter ensued as the album went around the square once more. Mary Beth suggested they talk to Norma at the post office since she'd lived in Stony Point all her life and might remember who the boy was. After a few minutes of discussion, Mary Beth clapped her hands. "Okay. Fun is fun, but we've got a big event coming up that needs our attention. Kate, I'll need you to help me with inventory. We'll need more supplies for the fair."

Annie put the album back into her paisley bag along with the red sweater she was crocheting for Joanna. She was trying the difficult petite popcorn stitch that required careful concentration. John would get a blue one just like it. . .if she could master this one! The sweaters would wrap around their little bodies and remind them how much their grandma loved them.

But she couldn't forget the boy in the photographs. Had someone made him a sweater or a warm scarf for his neck? Had he known the sweetness of someone's care, the tender awareness that he was valued in the world? Something told her he had not been so blessed. No doting grandmother had loved him. Sadness swept over her as she left the company of her needlework friends.

— 4 —

L ost in thought, Annie wandered out of A Stitch in Time and was startled when Alice caught up with her on the sidewalk. "Where are you going?" she asked, placing a hand on her hip. "I thought we might have coffee like we usually do after the Hook and Needle meeting."

"Oh, I've had enough coffee for one day," Annie sighed.

"Or lunch?" Alice's shapely eyebrow rose in an inquiring arc.

"I should get back. I have chores." Annie heard herself sigh again and shrugged. "I guess I'm a little blue. I don't know why. Maybe it's just that I can't get that boy out of my mind. No one should be forgotten like that. Alone. No family, no friends who care. I'd probably be poor company for you today."

"You're never poor company to me," Alice said, hooking an arm through Annie's. "But I understand. We can do lunch another day. Maybe tomorrow?" She screwed up her face in that little pleading gesture that always made Annie laugh.

"Sure." Annie opened the back door of the Malibu and dropped her things on the back seat. She paused, car keys in hand. "Alice, did you think Mary Beth seemed different today? Sort of. . .I don't know. . .worried or something?"

"She's just all worked up about the fair. And she's had a lot on her mind, too, what with her mother being ill and all."

Annie's mind went quickly to the report of an invader in the house and a misplaced photo. Could Mary Beth be growing forgetful at sixty? She'd seemed distracted, but she had become animated once they began to discuss plans for the fair.

"What is it with her mother? Is it dementia?" she asked. As if that were not enough, she added to herself.

"I think so. Her general health has been good up to this point, but she's failing. I know Mary Beth is worried about her."

Annie knew what it was like to worry about loved ones. When her parents were far away on the mission field, she'd felt their absence like a physical weight on her heart. "That's so hard," she said.

"Yes, and there's no one to share the burden. Mary Beth has had the sole care of her mom for the past five years. And believe me, it's been no picnic. Beatrice Brock is one very demanding lady." Alice picked up her needlework case from the curb. "Well, I guess if you're going to do chores instead of lunch, I'll go home and tackle the laundry I've been saving up." She rolled her eyes and waved good-bye with a flutter of red-tipped fingers.

But Annie didn't go home. What she needed was a long cleansing walk along the ocean. She drove down to the harbor. She'd park her car and walk all the way home to Grey Gables; then tomorrow she could go back and claim her car or get Alice to take her.

Maine had its share of flora and fauna, but along the ocean the dominant feature was water—miles and miles of cobalt and aquamarine splendor stippled with whitecaps. An occasional breeze gentled the sun's rays and sent a salty spray to cool the skin. Wispy clouds dappled the sky, and ospreys wheeled and sang in the blue expanse. Distant boats moved in slow dignity, as if in praise, their sails spread like angels' wings.

She stopped to pick up shells, dropping them in her big striped purse, her "treasure sack." Maybe she would put them in the rock garden or take them home for John and Joanna. The homesickness set in afresh. How she missed them! LeeAnn and Herb, too. . .her family.

She began the ascent along the shore road leading up to Ocean Drive and Grey Gables, letting the bliss of rock and sea and sky envelope her. She wanted to drink it all in and not miss a drop. The largeness of the feeling washed over her, and she found herself strangely frightened. Life was fragile. There was no fountain of youth; you simply grew relentlessly toward old age.

She could hardly be considered old, could she? Had she changed that much since she was a girl at the Fourth of July celebration with Gram? She recalled the tradition everyone looked forward to. Before the fireworks but just after dusk, the band would strike up some lighthearted patriotic number, and children and adults alike would start whirling around the bunting-draped bandstand. When dusk began to fall, everyone would take to their blankets to watch for the first great burst.

Her favorite part of the celebration came before the

fireworks. While they waited for the pyrotechnics, nature gave her own extravaganza. Field and lawn would pulsate with fireflies, all lit up by the soft points of light like notes in music through the velvety dark. When the day was over, everyone went inside to their beds in a kind of hushed solemnity, aware that they had been touched by something rare and lovely.

She wanted to recapture it, but one couldn't really go back. Even if you did go back, it wasn't the same without the people who made a night or a life beautiful. But perhaps she was beginning to regain something she'd lost from her childhood right here in Stony Point. Alice had quickly taken her to her heart, and Mary Beth and the ladies of the Hook and Needle Club had welcomed her.

And then there was Ian, perhaps the one new friend she cherished most. He'd been such a rock when she first arrived, helping her to navigate the twists and turns of Stony Point life. He was the kind of mayor every city or town should have, someone whose agenda was people, not position or power.

Wayne had been such a man and more, she thought, as the mild breeze swept through her.

Experts said a person in grief went through stages: denial, anger, bargaining, and acceptance, though not always in the same order or for the same length of time. Some even repeated the whole process, taking years to come to terms with it. The fact was, she was still dealing with Wayne's death. Would it ever be over? Could she handle life alone?

She looked down at her sandaled feet through a sudden rush of tears. Warm grains of sand squeezed through her bare toes and then fell away in ruffled ease, settling once again among a host of other grains. Lost, indistinguishable—like the years and tears of life. She moved on more slowly. Something sparkled in her peripheral vision. Rarely did someone litter this beautiful shore. She paused, picked up a small, unlabeled glass bottle.

The sun highlighted snatches of incandescent color in the smooth glass; it was beautiful. And suddenly Annie recalled a lovely image penned by the biblical King David. In his sorrow he imagined that God saved his tears in a bottle, kept them as something too precious to waste. Was it true that even pain and loss could be transformed, redeemed?

She reached the iron-colored flagstones leading up to Grey Gables and began the ascent slowly, aware at that moment that she was, in fact, quite alone—a widow whose child was grown and gone—who had come to sort out another widow's belongings, to ponder once more the precious and the passing. No one would be waiting for her when she reached Grey Gables.

Boots appeared suddenly from beneath an azalea bush to watch her approach. She sat demurely with her tail wrapped around her immaculate white paws until Annie came to a halt at her side.

"Except for you, Miss Boots," she told her. "How nice of you to come down and meet me." She stooped to stroke her silken fur, but the cat seemed distracted. Spinning around once with her tail high in the air, Boots marched up the walk in front of her. Perhaps she was hungry. Annie sighed and stood to follow the cat home.

She stopped in midrise, too surprised to consider the

irony that she'd been given the cold shoulder by a cat! At the same moment, she realized that someone was standing on her lawn staring at the house. Boots scampered away toward the rock garden, tail swishing.

Annie had seen this man before. Yesterday. . . or was it the day before? He had stopped at the end of the block and stood looking up at Grey Gables. A tourist out to enjoy the flavor of the village? A builder intrigued by the Victorian structure's design? She shrugged and made her way up the walk.

The man turned as she approached and stood his ground calmly, hands in the pockets of his sharply creased trousers. They were charcoal in color, and the belt below his white polo shirt defined a physique most men in their forties would envy.

His profile revealed classic features, the jaw prominent and smooth. His sandy hair, only mildly touched with gray, took on a golden glow in the waning afternoon sunlight. What was he doing here?

"Are you looking for someone?" she asked, shifting her bag of shells to her other shoulder.

The voice in answer was mellow, baritone, cosmopolitan. "Does Elizabeth Holden still live here?"

She couldn't help herself. "Obviously, you're not from around here, are ya?" She laughed at the stereotypical Mainer's quip and set her bag on the ground.

"I'm not, actually," he said, a slow smile tugging at his mouth. He held out a hand. "Dorian Jones."

She took it, felt its cool strength. "Annie Dawson," she replied amiably. "Elizabeth was my grandmother. She's passed

away, and I'm here to settle her estate, see to her affairs."
His eyes were sort of brownish. No, they were golden—
or more like amber, and his hair was sharply trimmed around
his ears. She looked away from his too intense gaze, from
something magnetic in it, but when she again faced him,
the intensity had faded.

"Forgive me, Miss Dawson," he said. "I haven't been
back to Stony Point in a very long time." He looked up at
the house once more, his brows furrowed in contemplation
or something else. "I spent a summer here back when I was
a kid saving for college."

"Really?" Annie was intrigued.

"Your grandmother let me do some odd jobs to earn some
money. She was very kind to me. I wanted to thank her."
He stopped speaking, eyes intent on Grey Gables. Then he
looked at her somewhat too deeply for comfort. "I'm very
sorry for your loss."

She felt oddly like crying. She'd been missing Wayne,
mourning her lost youth, and now Gram's absence from her
life struck her anew. "Thank you," she said quietly.

She swallowed against the lump in her throat. "Where
are you from, Mr., er. . .Jones?"

"It's Dorian. Dorian Jones, and I'm from New York
mostly, though I do quite a lot of traveling."

"Are you vacationing in these parts?"

That dreamy look washed over him again as though
he were remembering something, or trying to. "I never
forgot this place," he said. "The ocean, the rocky coastline,
the cobalt sky. . .the kindness of people." He looked at her
when he said "the kindness of people," a smile starting and

quickly fading. His eyes remained intense and impenetrable as though something very sad lingered in their depths. "I needed a job, and your grandmother let me do some carpentry and repairs for her. I'm good with my hands."

He took them out of his pockets briefly, and Annie saw that they were large and well groomed but hardly the calloused hands of a workman. "Gram was always eager to help someone out," she said. When he said nothing immediately, she asked, "You still into carpentry?"

"Oh, no," he said quickly with a little laugh. "That is, only as an occasional hobby. Mind you, I enjoy it, but I'm actually an appraiser—a collector of antiques—which is why Grey Gables interests me so much."

He even knew the name of Gram's house. Impressive. Or had he talked to someone in town? "Really?" she said again, wondering why she was given to monosyllables with this rather elegant but mysterious man.

An amused sparkle softened the intensity of his face. "Really. I provide assessments and such for auction houses. Sotheby's and the like. I even do appraisals for the *Antiques Roadshow* now and then. I'm trained in gemology, but all kinds of antiques interest me."

If she was tongue-tied before, she was perfectly astounded now. "Really" was on the tip of her tongue once more, but she squelched it. "You mean like on television— the real *Antiques Roadshow*?"

He gave his light laugh again. "It's nothing as exciting as that. I work strictly behind the scenes, do research on items people bring to the show. Believe me, I'm no television personality."

But he certainly could be, Annie thought, judging by his remarkable good looks, though perhaps he lacked a certain enthusiasm or gregariousness. There was an aloof manner about him or perhaps a sadness that held back the release of his full charm. No doubt he was somewhere in his forties; it was hard to tell where exactly. He certainly dressed well.

Those unusual eyes of his kept moving, darting from the house to the ocean to her and back to the house again. Restless, alert to detail. . .an appraiser's eyes, she supposed. Still, such restive motion made her feel peripheral somehow, left her wondering what he was seeing that she could not.

"I don't remember Gram mentioning anyone named Dorian," she said, trying to gather her wits about her. "Actually, it's a name I haven't heard since high school literature. You know, *The Picture of Dorian Gray*. Oscar Wilde's novel. Do you remember it? The character is willing to sell his soul if only the picture would grow old instead of him. It's interesting, isn't it? Dorian Gray. . .you're Dorian and this is Grey Gables."

She waited for his response to her witty reflection, but when it didn't come, she continued, "I used to come here as a child. I visited Gram every summer for a while. We might even have been here at the same time. How long ago were you here?"

"Gosh," he said. A most uncosmopolitan word. And he seemed to cast about in his memory. "Decades, I'm afraid. Can't recall exactly. It was only one summer. . ." He paused. "But it was a memorable one, and I think your grandmother had a lot to do with it. Without her generosity, I'd probably never have made it through school. I think I have her to thank for my first affection for antiques."

"She might not take kindly to being called an antique. . . if she were here," Annie said.

He gave her a puzzled look. "Oh, sorry. I didn't mean her."

Even when he "got" the joke, though, he didn't laugh. This was a very tightly wound man, Annie decided. He definitely needed a vacation.

"Does your grandmother. . .that is, did your grandmother keep that beautiful rococo table? The one with the fleur-de-lis apron?"

Annie gasped. He must mean Gram's prized table that sat in the living room just beneath the grand bay window. How odd that he would remember. How strange to feel tied to this stranger who knew something about her while she knew nothing about him. It was unnerving and at the same time oddly engaging.

How sweet it would be to talk about Gram with someone who'd known her long ago. Perhaps she should ask him to sit down on the porch. There was no car in sight, so he must have been walking for some time. But as red flags began waving in her mind, Dorian Jones straightened, drew in his breath, and released it slowly.

"You've got a great house here. You've inherited a real keeper." And he started away abruptly, his long, loose stride soundless on the flagstones. He took a few steps and turned. "I hope we'll run into each other again. I'll be around most of the summer. I'm at the Maplehurst."

And he was gone. Just like that. No good-byes, no

suggestion that they might talk again. She couldn't tell if she was relieved or disappointed. Taking a whole summer off, she mused. He had to be quite successful to put everything on hold and go off to the rocky coast of Maine just to relive one summer and to look up an old woman who'd given him a job.

A successful man could be a powerful draw for a woman. She knew that much after all these years. She knew too that she was far too vulnerable at this point in her life to consider any relationship with a man. Even a tall handsome stranger who was tied somehow to the grandmother she loved and cherished.

And why did she think she even had anything to consider? He had said what he came to say, and he'd gone. Annie climbed the porch steps, opened the door, and dropped her crochet tote in the hall. Before the door flapped shut, Boots scrambled through it and perched on the step leading upstairs.

"Well, you were some hostess, Miss Boots," she commented. Boots was usually quite a social creature for a cat. When Emma Watson had come by to sell Avon, Boots had nearly given the woman a heart attack. The little scamp had jumped up in the middle of her broad lap, sending her brochures and fragrant samples flying. Today she'd been anything but the contented lap cat. "A gentleman comes to call, and you make yourself scarce. Aren't you ashamed?"

But Boots merely stared at her through disapproving yellow slits, the tip of her curled tail moving slowly up and down.

— 5 —

Wednesday morning Mary Beth smoothed the chenille bedspread and set the small, decorative pillows at precise angles against the headboard. She liked order in her home, especially after a busy day at the shop. Yesterday the Hook and Needle Club had rallied around her idea for a craft fair. It had been a good day. She had yet to speak to Ian about it; they needed his support if the venture was to succeed. Suddenly the phone on her bedside table rang.

"Miss Brock? This is Susan Rigsby at Seaside Hills."

Mary Beth felt her breath catch in her throat. What now? Her aging mother had been fairly content at the assisted living center, especially as the dementia worsened and she'd stopped demanding continuous red carpet treatment. Dementia had actually left her mother a nicer person. It was shocking but true.

Mary Beth often reflected on the irony of her imperious New Yorker mother living in Stony Point, "a middling little village on the edge of nowhere." That's how the eighty-eight-year-old Beatrice Bennington Brock had referred to her eldest daughter's adopted community. "How can you stand it? All that folksy riff-raff and not a decent mall for miles!" Of course she was wrong; a quite adequate mall had been built on the outskirts of town. But a woman convinced against her will is of the same opinion still.

"Your mother's not in immediate danger," the voice, soft and professional, continued, "but she's having some trouble breathing. The doctor wants to step up the oxygen so she's on it during the night and several hours during the day as well."

Mary Beth sat down heavily in the wing chair by the phone. She drew in her breath and released it slowly. Her mother's respiratory infection had held on persistently, and pneumonia was a constant threat. "I see," Mary Beth said wearily. "I'll come by this afternoon."

She put the handset down into its cradle but made no move to get up from the chair. Everyone commented about her "indomitable energy, her effervescent spirit," but just now she was feeling every second of her sixty years.

She'd made all the arrangements for her mother's move to Stony Point. Her mother could no longer manage on her own, and there was no one but Mary Beth to look after her. Well, no one who was *willing* to assume the burden of an aging parent with progressive dementia. In the past five years, she had monitored everything relating to her mother's care at Seaside Hills. She'd visited faithfully, enduring endless complaints and comparisons, tiresome observations. "Your sister Melanie has really made a name for herself. Her fashion line is right up there with the top designers." Or, "Melanie would positively despair over these hideous drapes!" Or. "This bedspread looks like it came from the second-hand store."

Mary Beth knew her mother disapproved of her. Sometimes her appraisals were silent, but not often enough. "Are those overalls you're wearing?" Mary Beth was tempted to wear the scruffiest, most outrageous outfit she owned just to irritate her. She hadn't, of course. At least not on purpose. The woman was still her mother.

Mary Beth sighed. She caught a glimpse of herself in the mirror and realized she was shaking her head. She stopped and frowned into the image. Who was that looking back at her? When had she gotten so old? For heaven's sake, wasn't sixty the new forty?

She gazed at her roundish face with its crop of salt-and-pepper hair. She cut it faithfully every four weeks and in between hardly gave it a second thought. How long ago had she brushed long, chestnut locks that hung well below her shoulders? Was that in another life? Even into her thirties she could still arrange it in a single braid and flip it over her shoulder.

"Let's see. That would be B.C.," she mumbled. Before Clyde. She laughed a little at her thought, but the sound held no mirth. How many times had she promised herself she would wipe him irrevocably from her memory? Yet here she was nearly three decades later thinking of him. That they'd never married she saw now as a blessing. . .or a curse. What would it have meant to have a child of her own?

Well, life wasn't all bad, she reflected. She stared at her brown eyes looking out from beneath untended brows sprouting hairs she was usually too busy to pluck. But for Clyde she might never have come to Stony Point, never had the gumption to get out from the domination of her mother and the Brock dynasty.

Well, it wasn't a dynasty exactly. But pressure to buy into her mother's fashion world with its glamour and greed had been formidable. That life had never appealed to her. So much in life interested her more than clothes and making good impressions on the rest of the world. She'd failed to be drawn in, unlike her gorgeous but grasping sister, Melanie.

As children, she and Melanie had played dress-up. They'd try on discarded hats from their Mother's warehouse. . .hats with great plumes and exotic flowers. They'd laugh until their sides ached. Yes, those had been good days with Melanie. Before avarice had turned her witty little sister into the ultimate material girl.

Melanie had made good in the family business. At fifty-eight she still traveled the globe looking for conglomerates eager to purchase Bennington-Brock designs. She had made two failed personal alliances, produced a child, Amy, and now lived alone in an upscale Manhattan apartment that cost in a month more than her shopkeeper sister made in six months. The design company, too, had evolved and was known now simply as "Melanie."

Mary Beth rose from the wing chair, eager to escape the mirror's magnetic pull into memories best left buried. Her back hurt from stooping over and digging through materials at her shop. Even with Kate's help, a lot was yet to be done. Perhaps she'd been foolish to plan a needlework fair now that her mother's health was declining. She sighed. She might just want to curl up and blow away if she didn't have A Stitch in Time and her Hook and Needle friends. Old friends, like Stella and Gwen, and new ones like the warm-hearted, energetic Annie.

Yes, her little shop was her lifeline. When Clyde had left her for greener and younger pastures, she'd gotten into her big boat of a Buick and literally fled the city. She'd always loved the rocky coast of Maine, and Stony Point had charmed her instantly. She found a little cottage a few miles from town center and spent the bulk of her trust fund to buy the shop. Somewhere along the line she'd traded in her Buick for an SUV.

How she loved being surrounded by spools of rainbow thread and skeins of multicolored yarn waiting to be transformed by creative minds and hands! Now she fairly yearned for the shop's wooly comfort. She rinsed her coffee mug in the sink, dried it, and then neatly hung the towel back on its rack. Her personal life might be chaotic but at least her house and shop would maintain careful order.

She grabbed her slicker and her keys. Rainy or not, she liked to wear the shiny yellow jacket with its luminous color and patina. It lifted her spirits. And today she needed a lift.

Ian was just stepping out of the Cup and Saucer when she pulled up to A Stitch in Time. Even more than her yellow slicker, Ian could bring the sun out. "Top of the morning!" she called. Hardly Maine jargon and she wasn't Irish, but she liked the ring of the phrase.

"Good morning to you, Mary Beth." He helped her out of the SUV, sweeping one arm like Sir Walter Raleigh, and she felt like laughing for the first time since she'd gotten out of bed that morning.

Mayor for more years than she could remember, Ian wasn't your usual politician. When he kissed a baby, he did it with real affection; when he had a hard decision to make that was likely to anger someone, he agonized over it.

Oh, if she were only ten years younger and twenty pounds lighter!

"I've been meaning to talk to you about something, Ian," she said, hooking her arm through his. "I want to hold a craft fair to show off the needlework of the ladies of the club. And I want it to be big. Really big! We want to hold it in the town square." She felt her pulse race as she thought about it.

"Hold on, girl!" Ian said, laughing. "When is this shindig supposed to happen? We'll have to. . ."

"August 10, and we're going to get all the merchants in town involved and we think it would be great to have an auction. We'll sell off some white elephants from people's attics. . .Gwen's getting her society friends to buy in, and Annie has promised a Betsy Original and. . . Oh, I'm sorry. I'm talking your leg off."

Ian was shaking his head reflectively, and the crinkles at the corners of his eyes deepened. "I can see you've got your mind made up, Mary Beth. Well, if anyone can pull it off, you can. I'll run it by the town council. Don't think there'll be a problem. . .except maybe rain on the tenth of August."

"No rain. I've put my order in, but if it does, the bandstand is covered, and we can move into the community center at the church. That room will be perfect. As a matter of fact, I think that might be a good place to display all the needlework items. And outside we can have concessions. You know, hot dogs, lemonade, popcorn. And we'll hold the auction in the bandstand!"

"You're a wonder, Miss Brock," Ian said. He grew quiet and seconds later began rattling the coins in the pockets of his beige slacks, with that look on his face that said he had important business on his mind.

Actually, Mary Beth thought as she looked up at him, he seemed more preoccupied than usual, even troubled. He looked drawn and tired, as though he hadn't slept well. "Not worried about this, are you, Ian?" she asked more quietly.

"Oh, no. Sorry. I'm sure it will be a grand event with you at the helm." But the little furrow on his brow hadn't relaxed.

"Everything all right, Ian?" she asked. She'd known him for more years than she could count at the moment, and she suspected something was amiss.

"Everything's fine. . .here in the village, but. . ." He left the sentence hanging, and the furrow deepened.

She waited, watching the little muscle work at his left temple.

"Well, whenever I hear of illegal activity in our fair state, I get nervous." He sighed, shrugged. "There's been some talk of trouble down the coast, mostly south of Portland. A long way from here, but. . .well, we have to keep our eyes open."

He clapped Mary Beth's shoulder as though to apologize for sounding a note of gloom in the midst of her apparent happiness. "Good luck with your plans. And don't worry. The town council will know a good thing when they see it." And he was off, his long stride full of purpose.

Mary Beth unlocked the door to A Stitch in Time and immediately felt a kind of peace come over her. Last year she'd purchased new wall units. And she'd bought shiny new peg baskets for grouping skeins by color and type:

the bouclés, the merino wools, an infinite variety of other popular yarns. She stocked a wide variety of thread, too, including rayon, cotton, polyester, tweeds, and metallics. She also carried the best embroidery and quilting needles available.

Kate had polished the glass-topped counters until they gleamed. Since her divorce, she'd given more time to the shop and also to her own creativity. Her handmade jackets, most of them crocheted, were works of art. So was her patience with newcomers to the craft. She was even teaching Vanessa to crochet. Somehow she'd convinced her teenaged daughter that it was not a quaint anachronism and that the coolest of modern twenty-first century women could benefit from needlework.

Mary Beth went straight to the coffee maker in the back of her shop. The call from Seaside had derailed her, and she had left the house after only one cup of her favorite French roast. Later she would leave Kate in charge of the shop and head for Seaside Hills. She frowned, wondering what to expect when she saw her mother.

"She's not in danger," Susan had said over the phone, "just having a bit more trouble breathing." How could trouble breathing be anything but dangerous? In recent months she'd felt something very near love for the aging fashion mogul who'd seldom had time for her before but now had nothing but time. How much more time did her mother have?

She should call Melanie. Not that her sister didn't know exactly where her mother was and that the dementia was worsening. Susan at Seaside would have alerted

Melanie about the pneumonia, too. The arrangement was a convenient one since Melanie wanted as little to do with her Stony Point sister as possible. If there was a change in Mother's condition or something pressing, Susan left word for Melanie. Her sister might fly in, rent a car, and go straight to Seaside Hills without a word for Mary Beth, let alone a visit. In the past five years, Melanie had come all of three times.

"That's pretty sad!" Mary Beth said aloud, and looked around nervously. Was she talking to herself now? She sipped her coffee, relishing the hot strength of it. She thanked God for her friends in Stony Point and for the Hook and Needle members who were really the only sisters she had. They buoyed her up when the day-to-day needs of her mother wore her down.

Still, when it came right down to it, Mary Beth carried the load alone on her shoulders.

"Can you come and talk to your mother? She's refusing to eat, and if she doesn't we'll have to consider other options."

"Your mother's dumping clothes in the wastebaskets along the corridors. Soon she'll have nothing left to wear."

Such calls had been frequent, and as always, there was only Mary Beth to run interference. She sighed. She knew she wasn't the only caregiver whose family members left one sibling to carry the load. Nor was she the only one robbed of a sister through some misunderstanding.

Misunderstanding? Mary Beth shuddered. It was a lot more than that. It had placed a wedge between her and Melanie. . .and the niece she loved so dearly, too.

"Mary Beth? You here?" Kate Stevens peered tentatively around the corner. She gave Mary Beth one of her easy smiles. Some might judge Kate to be timid or weak. And perhaps it was true that she'd indulged Harry's drinking far too long. It had wreaked havoc on the family. But Kate had taken a stand and was gradually recovering from the pain of separation from the man she admittedly still loved.

Kate wore sleek black slacks and a white blouse under a chic purple crocheted jacket with satiny frog closures. It was the perfect color for the glossy dark hair fluffed softly around her face. She carried a small black purse that matched her low-heeled shoes. She loved purses and seemed to have an infinite variety. They were always a source of interest to Mary Beth, who never carried a purse herself. Her wallet fit nicely in the pocket of her slicker or smock.

"Thanks for all your work yesterday," Mary Beth said. "You can positively see your face in the counters. Does your back ache like mine after all that inventory work?"

"No, I'm fine," Kate said with a patient smile.

But Kate would never complain, even though there was still more counting to be done. "Kate, I hope you don't mind, but I've got to run over to Seaside Hills. My mother is. . ." She broke off. Was it a slip? A premonition? She'd been about to say "dying."

"Oh, I'm sorry. Is she ill? I mean other than the usual?" Kate put a hand on her arm, her gentle touch warming right through her sleeve.

"Well, no, not really, but the doctor is stepping up her oxygen. And of course it's difficult because sometimes she pulls out the oxygen tubing when she forgets or gets upset. You know how she is."

Kate's dark eyes reflected compassion. She'd listened patiently when Mary Beth came back from Seaside Hills with tales of some of her mother's ludicrous escapades. "You take as much time as you need. I can stay."

"Bless you, Kate." And Mary Beth was astonished to find herself near tears for the first time in years.

— 6 —

Annie pulled along the curb as close as she could get to Mike Malone's Hardware. The town center was already showing signs of heightened activity as visitors joined the locals on carefully kept streets. Stony Point was a quiet, proud town that took care of its own, but it welcomed the summer people with open arms. Besides raising its revenue every year, the tourists were interesting and most of them well-behaved and friendly.

The town square had been resurfaced and the grassy areas carefully manicured. Flowers blossomed in neatly spaced beds or freshly painted tubs from one end of Main Street to the other. She passed the Cultural Center where several cars with out-of-state plates had already parked in the lot. Strategically located across the street stood the white, colonial-style Maplehurst Inn with forest green trim and gleaming brass door handles.

She had driven by slowly and idly checked license plates on the closest cars. Of course there would be more than one New York plate. She hadn't really been looking for Dorian Jones. Had she? She had to admit she'd been touched by the way he'd looked deeply into her eyes and spoken of her grandmother. What had the two shared so long ago? And why was it so important for him to return to thank her? And would she, Betsy Dawson's granddaughter, see him again?

"Morning, Mike," she called. The store wasn't a big tourist draw, but it too would get its share of the gawk-and-geek crowd that had had enough of Menard's and Home Depot and wanted a look at a real small-town hardware store. Its only customer was a young man in jeans and T-shirt. At the counter he paid for a faucet handle and left without the proffered bag.

"What can I do you for?" Mike quipped. As usual, he turned the "you" and "for" around. He was an amiable fifty-ish Mainer with thinning brown hair and a small mustache. Medium height. Not an ounce of fat on him. Maybe that's what having five children in college did to a man! He wore dark trousers and his signature white shirt with a plastic name tag reading "Malone's" affixed to the pocket. The first time they'd met, she'd expected his outfit to come with a bow tie, but Mike's lean, tanned neck was free of any such encumbrance.

"I need something to fix window screens. The ones at Grey Gables are brittle and some of them have holes big enough for a squirrel to climb through."

"Gotcha," he said. "How much?"

"I don't know. You're the proprietor."

"I mean how much screening? Then I'll tell you how much it costs," he said smiling.

"Of course." Where was her head this morning?

"Well. . ."

"Uh, yes. How much? Well, I don't know exactly."

"How many screens do you have?" he asked patiently.

One thing she knew about Mike Malone was that he bent over backward to be helpful, especially to the many single women who cared for properties in the village. How many screens? She mentally added up the injured, which she'd set out on the porch for triage. Some were "definitely code blue" and others "patch, if possible." And then there was the fact that she didn't really have a clue about how to do the job. But how hard could it be? It wasn't rocket science, was it? "About six, I think. Yes, I'll start with six. What do I need?"

Mike led her toward rolls of plastic by the yard, weather stripping, and screening, his rubber-soled shoes squeaking mildly on the floor. "Well, you'll need a good wire-cutting scissors and a staple gun, plus the screening, of course. You've got those old wooden frames, right?"

"Right." Someday soon, sell or stay, she'd have to look into new windows. Some spiffy new double-glazed ones would increase Grey Gables' value. But for now she'd fix the old as best she could.

"Wally didn't tell you what to get?" he asked, releasing the wide, meshy scroll. "He's going to do the screens, isn't he?"

"Wally's laid up for a while. Broke his arm falling out of a tree. But I can't wait. I want to be able to open the windows and let in that marvelous sea breeze without entertaining the entire insect population."

Mike measured and cut, rolled and tied the materials, occasionally providing a tip or two he thought might be useful. "The Internet could give you step-by-step instructions, but if you get in a bind, give me a call. I'll try to walk you through it. Mind you, it can be tricky. It all depends on the condition of the frames."

Mike took her purchases out to the Malibu while she waited at the counter to pay. Now that was definitely an anachronism. Where else but in Stony Point would your goods be handed over before you paid the bill?

Casually, she inspected the somewhat cluttered counter while Mike was out. A mug of red and white "Malone's Hardware" pens, a display of Murphy's Soap ("for the down and dirty man"), and a few copies of *The Point* that looked fresh and new. *The Point* was nothing spectacular. In his spare time, Mike set up occasional issues of the newspaper in his computer and ran copies off on the Cultural Center's mega-memory, mega-color, do-everything-but-make-coffee printer. And there it was on the front page; Mary Beth hadn't wasted any time.

"A Stitch in Time will sponsor a needlework fair August 10. Local needlework artists will display and sell handwork in a variety of forms. Booths will be set up in the town center, along with concessions for all your favorite area snacks and treats. In conjunction, an auction will be held at the town bandstand across from the square. Antiques from Maine and beyond will be available for sale at the right price. A share of the proceeds will benefit the local food pantry at Stony Point Community Church."

"I see you've been wearing your reporter's hat," she said when Mike came back. "Can I take one?"

"Sure. That's what they're there for. And good luck with your window screens."

Later at Grey Gables, Annie dropped down with utter and complete exhaustion on her wicker chaise. She had spent the rest of the morning with no luck but bad. With several split wooden frames and bleeding fingers, she knew she'd have to admit temporary defeat and do what she should have in the first place: read the directions.

She took a deep breath and looked to the green canopy of trees for solace. The breeze whipped up bits of debris from her failed project, and the weak sun surrendered completely to a thick cloud cover. The distant ocean was dappled with white caps. Boots, who had "helped" by batting around the strips of curling mesh, leaped up on the storage trunk and demurely surveyed the battle scene.

"Some help you were," she scolded mildly. She was met with an imperious grin and a narrowing of almond eyes. "So I'm not a candidate for the 'compleat handywoman.'"

Her cell phone buzzed and she reached for it with her bandaged hand. "Ouch."

"Hello to you too," came Alice's familiar voice. "I'll try to make it quick and painless."

"Sorry. I nicked a couple of fingers. Should have grabbed the phone with the other hand."

"You sound awful. Do you need a ride to the emergency room?"

"No, but where were you when I needed you? I've been trying to repair some broken screens, and I guess I should have taken a cue from Mike. It's not as easy as it sounds. Maybe I'll have to wait for Wally's arm to heal or find someone else."

"Poor girl. Can I run over? You're not in bed or anything?"

"I nicked my finger; I didn't fall off a cliff. I'll put the tea on." She rang off, feeling better for hearing Alice's voice.

Obviously she had forgiven her for declining lunch after Tuesday's club meeting. And she'd been kind enough to take her back to the harbor to retrieve her car.

Alice appeared, bearing her needlework bag and a loaf of something that smelled like cinnamon. Alice had an uncanny natural talent for baking; everything she tried turned out beautifully shaped and altogether delicious. "Happy Homemaker here," she announced, letting herself in. "Good grief, what did you do to yourself?"

Annie looked down. Three fingers of her left hand sported bandages. Orange with happy faces, the only ones she could find. Maybe Gram had found them on sale. She stared at them ruefully. "Think of them as the latest thing in finger art. Peggy may want to do her nails this way."

"Go sit," Alice ordered. "I'll finish this. Where's your bread knife?"

Moments later they rejoined Boots, who politely removed herself from the porch, giving Alice the chair she had formerly occupied. Quietly, they savored the steaming tea and flavorful bread. A mild breeze stirred the sugar maple trees brushing the side of the house. They watched a few brave boats sail by on a somber ocean that reflected muddy skies. It had been overcast most of the day, which of course had saved her from repairing screens under a toasty sun. Make that trying to repair them.

"Saw the latest issue of *The Point* today, hot off the press," Annie said. "Mary Beth wasted no time getting the word out about the needlework fair. 'Concessions with all your favorite area treats. Antiques from Maine and beyond.' When our lady of Stony Point makes up her mind, she does it in a big way! Do you think we'll be ready by the tenth of August? We're well into June already."

"We'll have to get moving on the concessions, especially if we want merchants to donate things. July will be here before we know it." Alice drew her knees up on the wicker chair and sighed contentedly. "There's something so healing about the ocean, don't you think? I wonder how people in land-locked communities stand it. How was your walk yesterday?"

"I can't say it was exactly healing. More like penetrating." Annie recalled how lonely she had felt toward the end. How she had been gripped by a sense of rapidly passing years and her own dwindling mortality. "I collected some great shells for John and Joanna though. My best find was a sparkling white two-inch clam with deep, showy grooves."

"It must be wonderful having kids to buy for, to surprise with special things."

"Hmm," Annie assented. "I got something of a surprise myself when I got back to the house."

"Oh?" Alice leaned forward, her auburn hair draping one delicate shoulder.

"This guy was standing over there." Annie pointed to the rock garden where the lawn sloped down toward the street. "He was just standing and looking up at Grey Gables like it was some famous landmark or something. And the funny thing is, he was also here a few days earlier, looking up at the house then too. Is Grey Gables so unusual? Do you think I ought to charge admission? Maybe turn it into a bed and breakfast?"

"You mean that tall, good-looking guy with the muscles?"

Annie raised her eyebrows. Trust her to notice a handsome stranger. Alice had liked being married to John, even though he'd broken her heart more than once. How often could a woman's heart break before she'd give up on a man?

"I saw him looking up here," Alice said, her voice rising as it always did when she got excited. "I'd gone out for the mail and couldn't help but notice. I wasn't spying. Really. But I wish he'd been looking my way. Who was he? What did he want?"

Annie pursed her lips. "His name is Dorian Jones. He says he worked for Gram one summer back in the eighties to earn money for college. Says he always wanted to come back to Stony Point to thank her. He asked for Elizabeth Holden, and he knew the name Grey Gables." She paused, remembering the restless gaze that had stirred something needy in her. "Alice, do you remember anyone like him working for Gram?"

"Gosh, I'm sure I'd remember him if I'd seen him. It would have been more than two decades ago, wouldn't it? How old do you think he is?"

Annie had puzzled about Dorian's age, and she'd seen him pretty close up. The little lines in his forehead and around his mouth said late thirties, early forties; his eyes looked older, unless perhaps he'd been through some trauma that could age a man before his time. "I'm not sure. Forty maybe. Could be more."

"So. . .he's on vacation or what?" Alice asked eagerly.

"Says he's taking the summer off to enjoy the ocean, the village, and its 'kind people.' "

"A-hah!" Alice intoned. "That sounds like a come-on. I bet he was looking into those kind green eyes of yours and getting lost in them."

"Oh, stop!" Annie said. "It was nothing of the sort. He's just doing what every other tourist does. Getting away from it all and relaxing from a hectic lifestyle."

"And what kind of hectic lifestyle does Wonder Boy have?"

"Well, here's the surprising thing. He's some kind of expert in antiques. Does research and appraisals for auction houses. He even mentioned Sotheby's and the *Antiques Roadshow.*"

Alice opened her mouth and shut it again. She took a sip of her tea. "Wow. Well, maybe that could explain his interest in Grey Gables. Imagine what your grandmother would think if she knew some kid she'd given a job to had become a real success story! Sotheby's, for heaven's sake!"

"Did Gram ever say anything to you about kids who worked for her?" Gram and Alice had been close during the years Annie was absent. She'd helped her through her divorce and become a real mentor to her. No doubt they had shared experiences and memories. They'd both been lifelong Stony Point residents.

Alice shook her head slowly. "No, but you know how your Gram was. If anybody was in need, she was there to help. She might have had teenagers working for her. I think I'd remember someone who looked like him!"

Boots leaped up on the trunk at that moment, barely avoiding a half-filled cup of tea, and perched sedately on top of the photo album. At Annie's cry of alarm and quick rebuke, the cat jumped down again and trotted off to the other end of the porch. Annie brushed off the album, though Boots was a careful groomer and seldom shed her gray hairs.

"I've looked through this album several times, but I don't see anyone who looks like Mr. Dorian Jones," Annie said, thumbing slowly through the pages. Once again she was arrested by the serious young boy hanging about on the edges of the pictures. In one shot he was leaning on a huge rock several feet from a group of kids. Tanned and wiry, his small features were fixed in a secretive half smile. In another picture, he was standing with arms folded over his lean stomach, the sleeves of his shirt rolled up high on his scrawny arms.

"Maybe your mystery boy and the antiques appraiser are one and the same," Alice said with amusement in her voice. "And he's come back to haunt you!"

"Mr. Jones is blond," Annie said. "And the complexion is all wrong." She tapped her finger on the photo and squelched a spasm of pain from her poor pricked fingers. "Besides, this boy is small boned. His features are delicate, almost elfin. I think he could be Hispanic."

"Well, you can never tell from pictures. Shadows and faded color and all that. And besides, ever hear of hair dye for men?"

Annie sighed. She frowned into the dark, intriguing eyes in the photo. And it seemed to her that those eyes were looking deeply into hers, wanting to tell her something, pleading for her attention. She had to find out who he was.

"You really care about this boy, don't you?" Alice asked softly, her blue eyes wide.

"I do. Not sure why. There must have been a lot of teenagers around Stony Point two decades ago, but for some reason this one bugs me. I even dreamed about him. Now that's weird." Annie shook her head in wonder at herself.

"Well, why don't we go into town and look up some of the old *Points* from back then. There might be a story or two that will point us in the right direction. I'll help you." She paused to smile reassuringly at Annie. "I must say, though, I'm more interested in your new friend. Dorian, was it? Haven't heard that name since high school English."

"You're impossible!" Annie gave her friend a playful punch. "But thanks for the offer to help me look for him." She pressed her left hand over the page showing the boy peering out to sea. "Let's do it tomorrow." She sighed then as her wounded fingers began once more to throb. "Besides, I have to go to town to buy some more screening."

— 7 —

Mary Beth steered her SUV up the road that led to
Seaside Hills Assisted Living. The continuing care
retirement community offered lifestyle options to suit both
current and future health care needs. When her mother had
first arrived, she had lived in a section that provided limited
daily care; now she received skilled nursing in the Alzheimer's/
dementia section.

Mary Beth's thoughts rambled. Why had it happened? Why
to her mother? This woman whose sharp mind had launched
a flourishing business? "Deprived of mind," the meaning of
the word "dementia" held terrible images. So much remained
unknown, unclear about the various causes and manifesta-
tions of the disease. Nor was it any discriminator of persons,
often attacking those with high intelligence.

She found a premium spot in the visitors' parking area
and tried not to think about what lay ahead. She was tired,
and she still ached from the grueling inventory she and Kate
had completed. How would her mother be today? Would she
even know her?

Visits here were seldom pleasant. It was hard to see
people who had once been vibrant and active in their homes
and communities no longer able to care for themselves. And
sometimes, as logic gave way to distortion, penetrating wails
and heartrending cries echoed in the hallways. Once a dear

old man had flung his skinny arms around her and hung on with the tenacity of a bulldog, all the while weeping with joy to have found his long-lost mother.

Even the serenity of the ocean shimmering benignly in the sun could not always calm a troubled heart. The view from the top of Elm Street was nothing short of spectacular, over the roof tops of the village of Stony Point and down to the ocean beyond, where sailboats glided gently by. Sometimes she brought her mother to the wide patio where she could look out on the splendid vista without being battered by the wind. Mary Beth would pray that peace might descend, if only for a little while.

She nodded to the receptionist inside the spacious foyer, where a huge Oriental carpet of jade green and gold softened the institutional aura. Lamps and soft chairs were scattered around the room; pastoral paintings adorned the walls. One could almost imagine a hotel lobby but for a quick glance down one of the hallways extending from the foyer like spokes of a wagon wheel.

She took the second corridor on her right, hoping no alarming noises would come. Nor did she turn to look inside any of the open doors. She walked quickly, her rubber-soled shoes making no sound, until she came almost to the end of the hallway. Room 18.

The door was partially open. Mary Beth knocked anyway, hesitating briefly before entering. She shivered, though the temperature in the place was warm enough to hatch chickens.

The woman propped up on pale pink sheets, her white hair a wispy halo, turned slowly. The oxygen tubing had been set aside—an off hour for oxygen. Beatrice Bennington Brock was breathing quietly on her own. Though she had grown smaller with age, she still gave the impression of regal bearing, even beneath the bedcovers. She was dressed in one of her famous silky blouses, beige, long sleeved, the two top pearl buttons open. Beneath the blanket and sheets she was probably wearing flannel or jersey knit pants.

The liquid blue eyes narrowed, widened, and narrowed once again. Then suddenly a smile broke across the wrinkled face. Mary Beth had dreamed of such a greeting from her mother, who seldom seemed glad to see her.

Tall. Imperious. Demanding. Those were the qualities for which Beatrice Brock was known. And perhaps in the fast-paced, competitive world of fashion design, those attributes were necessary for survival. But they did little to comfort a daughter who longed to be loved. Was it possible that now. . . ?

One thin arm, gnarled fingers curved, reached toward her. "Melanie? Is that you?"

Mary Beth dropped down heavily on the chair next to the bed. "No, Mother. It's me, Mary Beth." She tried to keep the disappointment out of her voice, though her mother wasn't apt to notice anyway. Being mistaken for her elegant sister was quite a stretch. It would be funny. . .if it weren't so sad.

The smile faded, but the watery eyes remained fixed, as though she were still trying to work out who was speaking to her.

Mary Beth patted her mother's arm and eased it back under the blanket. "How are you, Mother?"

"Oh," she said, her eyes roving over Mary Beth's face

and hair, her plain white blouse, denim skirt, and the yellow slicker she'd laid across the back of the chair. "Oh," she
said again. And she leaned back against the pillows, closing
her eyes.

Shut out once more, Mary Beth realized. Why did it still
hurt?

But suddenly the eyes opened. The regal head turned.
"Of course it's you," she said. "When did you get in?"

Get in? Did she imagine she was still in New York? That
Mary Beth had come home for a visit? She had visited rarely,
not only because she felt unwelcome but because her mother
was always off somewhere. And of course there was Melanie,
who had never forgiven her sister's "lack of insight and negli-
gence" that summer so long ago.

"Oh, I've been here right along, Mother. You're in Stony
Point, remember? And you and I visit regularly. Yesterday we
had lunch together."

The head turned fretfully on the pillows. "Why doesn't
anyone tell me these things?"

A young aide came in carrying a round tray with three
little white paper cups. She was blond and pert and wore
a teddy-bear smock over white pants. Pouring water from a
glass pitcher, she said, "Time for your meds, Mrs. Brock. I can
bring you some ginger ale too, if you like."

"Amy?" The faint eyebrows lifted, a smile spread across
the gaunt features as she looked into the face she perceived
as her granddaughter, Melanie's Amy.

"No. It's me, your aide Sherry. Here, let's raise you up a
bit." And she pressed a button that brought the top half of the
bed up.

Mary Beth moved away, busied herself straightening books and papers at the far end of the room. Her mother had one of the finer suites that included a small sitting area with soft chairs and two small tables. On one wall, a dresser bore a Victorian comb and brush set, a silver tray of brooches and buttons, and a few old photos.

In one infamous photo, she and Melanie showed off huge flowered hats, their chubby faces wreathed in smiles. Mary Beth's long curls, the color of dark taffy, mingled with her sister's golden ones. Their small arms were entwined around each other as they grinned for the camera. Melanie's two front teeth were missing. It's a wonder Melanie hadn't destroyed the photo when she last visited her mother. September, wasn't it?

"Honestly, Mary Beth, I just don't understand why you would want to hide yourself away in that godforsaken Rocky River or whatever!" The sting of Melanie's words remained after all these years.

She tore her eyes away and stepped to the other side of the dresser, where a young girl smiled out of a gilt-edged frame, her hair pale as champagne and fine as spun glass. Her eyes were blue like Melanie's, only lighter and silvery, as though touched by moonlight. Her unsmiling mouth was deeply pensive, as Amy had always been. It was the same photo of Amy she kept on her mantel at the cottage, precisely five inches from the Baroque mantel clock she'd ordered from Sedgewick's. In it Amy wore her high school graduation robe in the royal blue and gold colors of her school. Wide ruching and gold piping circled the girl's reed-like neck. The fine smooth hair curled under in a page-boy at her delicate shoulders.

Now in her late thirties, Amy was still beautiful, with those same troubled blue eyes. Raised amid wealth and family dysfunction, she'd been a lonely child. Not that the two always went together, but in Amy's case and in her own, Mary Beth realized, it was achingly so. Maybe that's why she and Amy had found a special bond, a bond that festered between Melanie and Mary Beth. It had been fun visiting Amy in New York in the early years of her childhood. They did the usual things: a cruise on the Hudson, lunch in Manhattan, visits to the harbor and the magnificent Lady Liberty. Sometimes just quiet evenings playing Chutes and Ladders or baking cookies. If she could have had a child, she'd want one just like Amy.

When Amy's junior high years came around, Mary Beth's visits were fewer. Different, too. Amy was preoccupied, moody, given to long solitary periods in her room. But Mary Beth continued to write her newsy letters, to send Amy little presents—a perfect starfish, a necklace made of shells, a book of Silverstein poems. For three years there were no visits. Then came that fateful summer when Amy had turned sixteen.

One didn't need to birth a child to love it. She sighed, turned away from the photo of Amy, and ventured back to her mother's side. The teddy-bear-smocked Sherry was gently reinserting the oxygen tubing into her patient's nose. She gave Mary Beth a professional smile and left the room, stopping at the wheel-driven cart with its laptop computer to make her entries.

Beatrice was settled back on the pillows, her eyes closed. Mary Beth sat next to her for a long time, listening to the sound of her mother's shallow, irregular breathing. She studied the narrow face. After a while the lines and furrows in its pale contours relaxed. Mary Beth had seldom seen her without that sharp, imperious, in-control expression with which she faced everyone. Her mother looked almost peaceful. Mary Beth felt an odd impulse to smooth the wispy hair back from the white forehead.

Beatrice was quiet a long while, though Mary Beth knew she was not asleep. What went on in that befuddled mind? What demon burrowed into the recesses of the hapless brain and twisted it? Blue-veined hands were folded over the little mound at her mother's waist. Her eyes opened and closed a time or two and then were still. Perhaps she would sleep after all.

Then, as though some altogether lovely thought had just occurred to her, Beatrice opened her eyes. She cocked her head to one side. Her lips opened. "You always were a good girl, my Mary."

Mary Beth felt her heart leap. No matter what terrors issued forth in days to come, she knew she would hold on to those words: "My Mary." Mary Beth leaned forward. She reached out trembling fingers over her mother's white brow and then drew them back into her lap again without touching her. She was asleep.

A slight rustle at the door caught her attention. Reverend Wallace raised a hand as though to knock, but stopped in midair, a question in his eyes. Mary Beth got up abruptly and went out, closing the door behind her. "She's just fallen asleep," she whispered, taking his arm and moving him down the hall.

"Ah, I see," he whispered back; then as they moved out of earshot he added more loudly, "I can come back tomorrow.

No need to disturb her. How is she?"

"I'm sorry you came for nothing, Reverend Wallace," she said, stepping out onto the patio. "I know my mother would have liked to see you. She's a little better today, I think." The fresh air swept through her lungs, adding to the headiness of her mother's remembered words: "My Mary." Heart soaring, she sat down in one of the wrought iron chairs and gestured for him to join her.

Reverend Roy Wallace was of medium height and wore a short-sleeved black shirt with black pants. A white collar encircled his neck. In his late sixties, he was what one might call portly, but never fat, and his energetic step was the envy of much younger men. It was hard to imagine Stony Point without him. His brown eyes held warmth and a kind of serenity that might just be contagious for all she knew.

"I'm delighted to hear it, Mary Beth," he said. "Now, tell me, how are *you*?" He tucked a small Testament into his shirt pocket and drew large hands together in his usual "I'm listening" posture.

"I am well, thank you very much. Mother has some tough days, and sometimes she's in a world I can't see, but today. . ." She broke off. How could she explain what those tender words from her usually critical mother meant? Could her elation be seen in her face? "You were right, Reverend Wallace. When times are hard, if we hold on, at some point the light that's always been hidden behind the gloom becomes visible."

"It's a wonderful truth," he said, tempering his voice that always had a bit of thunder in it. "The sun is shining even when we can't see it. And we can believe that God is there even when he seems silent or far away."

"She knew me today. Well, after a while, and she. . ." But it was not a thing she could share, even with this gentle minister she loved and respected. The experience was too personal, too deep. "She. . .uh. . .she and I had a good visit."

He leaned forward in his chair, and a strand of straight silver hair fell over his forehead; he thrust it back with a laugh. "That's first rate," he said. It was a favorite expression of his. If he'd enjoyed a particularly good dish at a church supper, he proclaimed it "first rate." If the day was fine, he declared it "first rate." His eyebrows went up in sudden thought. "By the way, I hear the ladies of your needlework club are cooking up a special event of some sort."

"A needlework fair," she supplied. "The ladies are going to display their work and we're going to have an auction and concessions too. Not sure what we'll do for an impartial judge and auctioneer, but we'll work on that. And, just to let you know, we're not forgetting what's important. There'll be a donation from the proceeds for the church."

"First rate," he said.

"I just hope. . ." She paused, wishing the thought didn't keep recurring. "I hope Mother can hold on. She's eighty-eight, and the breathing problem has us all a bit worried."

"Will some of the family be coming to visit your mother now? I haven't seen that niece of yours in a long time."

No doubt the "us" had made Reverend Wallace think of family. Of course, Melanie would come sooner or later and so would Amy, who was faithful to write or phone. But even after all these years, Amy wasn't comfortable in Stony Point. And now with Annie showing that photograph all around town, things could get out of hand.

"I. . .uh. . .I'm not sure." She felt her earlier lightness
trickle away. They would come eventually, and certainly
for a funeral. And then what? Something terrible had
happened the night that boy had disappeared, something
Amy even now wouldn't talk about. She rose from the chair
and grabbed her slicker. "I guess I'd better get back to the
shop. Kate will think I deserted her."

Reverend Wallace got up, too, and touched Mary Beth
under the elbow. "I'll look in on your mother tomorrow."

She nodded without moving, suddenly overcome with
a sense of dread. She was riding such a roller coaster of
feeling! A cloud of impending death had hung over her for
days, and then a dreaded visit had turned tender, almost
euphoric. A surge of hope and faith and then once more
this dark unknowing. She swallowed.

"You all right, Mary Beth?" Her minister's gentle
question nearly unhinged her. She'd been pushing down
thoughts of Amy for weeks, forcing away the memories of
that long-ago summer and what it had done to her niece.
Though years had rolled by, the vulnerable girl had never
really gotten past it. Perhaps they had been wrong to keep
silent, to push it all away.

"Yes. Yes, I'm fine. Forgive me, I've got to run." She turned
and, knowing she was being far too abrupt, called over her
shoulder, "Thanks so much for coming." She fled to the SUV
and roared down the hill.

8

Annie put on a light jacket over her blouse and white Capri pants. Mornings were often cool at Stony Point but by midmorning there would no longer be a need for outerwear. Alice had called to beg off going into town; she had a headache threatening to become a migraine. So Annie was preparing to go alone; the screens just couldn't wait.

She brushed her thick mop of sandy hair and noticed that the sun had begun to lighten it. Surely those were not streaks of gray she was seeing. She rubbed a bit of moisturizing gel into her scalp and thought of buying a hat. She was growing tan from walks along the coast and sunning on Grey Gables' porch. She liked the deeper color on her arms and legs, which she hoped really were toning up; she wasn't just imagining it, was she? She turned her head to one side, pondered her image in the mirror.

The face looking back at her from Gram's filigreed mirror showed heightened color that made her eyes seem greener. Or did they just reflect the emerald shade of her blouse? Light freckles dotted her short Holden nose. Gram's nose. Good thing she didn't need glasses; they'd never stay up on so small a buttress.

Wayne used to kiss the tip of her nose, she remembered with a sudden flash of clarity. She saw his face in heartrending detail; square and lean with gray eyes that were sometimes blue, sometimes hazel, with little crinkles at their corners that could never be dubbed "crow's feet." Annie could almost feel his strong hands on her shoulders, imagine his face looking over the top of hers. She turned away from the mirror and forced a light step on the stairs.

Boots was waiting at the bottom. How did she always know when her mistress was preparing to leave? "Be a good cat," she said, giving her a long stroke from head to tail. Boots had her own little trap door so she could go in and out. Gram's idea? Did she ever think that other critters could get in that way too? Were there skunks in Stony Point? Annie shivered and determined not to think about it.

She threw her jacket in the back seat and revved up the car's motor. It was fast becoming an antique, but how could she part with it for a newer model? It had been Wayne's gift to her one Christmas. Trading it in would be downright disloyal; besides, she loved the sweet old thing, rattles, twitters and all.

Rather than head straight for town, Annie decided to detour along the coastal road, Grand Avenue. Maybe she'd run into Wally down by the harbor and see how he was getting along. Yesterday's brooding sky had given way to brilliance. The sun shone on water so smooth that boats appeared to glide like skaters on ice. It was a shame not to open the windows and drink in the air, whether it blew her hair to kingdom come or not.

She found Wally on the dock, black hair gleaming nearly purple in the sun. He was wearing jeans and a shirt Peggy must have doctored to accommodate the heavy cast. But this time he wasn't sitting idly on the pier; he was holding a long black hose in his good right arm. A stream of water gushed onto the dock as the lobster shack got a thorough wash after yesterday's catch.

"Hey, Wally," she called, staying back from the gushing water.

He turned, shut off the spray and came toward her. She warmed to his rare smile; he was clearly not the same gloomy guy she'd seen last.

"Don't get too close," he called. "There's fish guts—and the dock's bound to be slick as a seal's belly."

The odor confirmed his colorful diagnosis. "Great morning," she said, as he came toward her. "How's the arm?"

He looked at the soiled cast, moved the heavy thing out from his body slightly. "Pain's not too bad mostly," he said. "Good thing. Got me a job. Well, ain't much of a job but it's okay. Keeps me from growing barnacles."

Annie felt a rush of gratitude. Ian had been as good as his word. Todd Butler ran one of the more successful fisheries and supplied not only the town's demand for lobsters but shipped them off by the thousands to points east and west. "How are Peggy and Emily?"

"Doing good. Thanks." He began to back up, kicking the hose out of his way. "Well, gotta' get to work."

The spark of pride in his voice touched Annie. She tried to picture Wally as the boy in her album, but Wally was clearly fair-skinned. She waved good-bye, delighting in Wally's change of mood and eager to thank Ian for once more stepping up to the plate for Stony Point's own.

Mike was busy with customers when she got to the

hardware store. She'd had to park down the block but left her windows open to keep her car from becoming a raging Inferno, especially if she planned to stay long enough to check for news items from the eighties in Mike's morgue. She shivered. "Morgue," a macabre name for a storehouse of old newspapers.

She browsed among the shelves while she waited for Mike, mentally rehearsing how she would describe her foray into the world of rescreening. There should have been enough for six windows, but she'd had to recut a few, and once she'd accidentally put her foot through one. If only Wally had left his sawhorses at Grey Gables. Maybe she'd have to invest in a couple. Meanwhile, a version of "the dog ate my homework" was not likely to hold much weight with anyone.

A man in a "Go Bears" shirt was buying some kind of cable, while no doubt alienating himself from a town full of New England Patriots. An elderly woman in red pants and a "Virginia Is for Lovers" sweatshirt paid for a carton of lightbulbs. Out of the corner of her eye Annie watched the woman exit. Then she approached the counter.

"Hi, Mike. Beautiful day!" she called brightly.

"Back again," he said. "How's the screen project coming? Done already?"

"Uh, no," she said with weary finality. "Actually, I need some clamps, something to hold one end while I'm working with the other. . ."

"Uh-huh," he said knowingly. "Slippery little devils, aren't they?"

"The slipperiest." She sighed. "I ruined at least a couple yards of screening. I never knew fixing screens could be so maddening!"

"It's one of the toughest chores, I think, Annie. Don't be too hard on yourself." Mike pulled at his left ear, an endearing little gesture she liked about him. "I wish I could come out myself and help, but when I'm not tied up here at the store, I'm dealing with Fiona's honey-do list."

"Thanks, Mike."

He came back and plunked several middle-sized steel things with long screws on the counter and set three rolls of screening on the floor. He began the tally.

The supplies were only one reason for coming into town that morning. She wanted to get his reaction to the mystery photo. "By the way. . ." She opened her purse and drew out a snapshot showing the young boy. She'd chosen a picture that most clearly showed the troubled face.

"What's this?" Mike asked casually as she handed him the photo.

"I found it in an album among Gram's things. Actually, there are several pictures of this boy in the book, but nobody seems to know who he is. You've been around Stony Point a long time. I thought you might have an idea."

Mike squinted and pulled a pair of readers out of his shirt pocket. He inspected the photo for several seconds. "Nope, can't say as I do."

Annie sighed and looked ruefully down at the photo on the counter. "I just thought you might remember him from an old edition of *The Point* or something. Gram saved a ton of pictures, and this guy showed up a lot." Annie turned around at the sound of the store's old-fashioned bell announcing a customer.

"I need a couple dozen of the latest *Points*," a familiar voice called.

Mary Beth Brock came barreling toward the counter, her sturdy shoes making little thudding noises on the vinyl tiles. Dressed in black denim jeans and her maroon Stitch in Time smock, she'd obviously run out of the store between customers.

"Hi, Annie," she said, catching her breath. She looked from Annie to Mike and down at the dark-haired boy in the photo. And it seemed to Annie that a shadow crossed the slightly flushed face. "I. . .I need to replenish my supply of. . ." She paused as though she'd briefly lost her train of thought. ". . .flyers for the needlework fair," she finished. Two red spots appeared on her round cheeks. Her eyes darted back and forth from the photo to Annie. "I hope you're hitting Mike up for several cases of something wonderful for the fair!" She reached out a plump hand. "All right if I take these?" She scooped up a small stack of flyers from the counter without waiting for Mike's response. "Gotta run. Thanks Mike. Nice seeing you, Annie."

Annie looked at Mike. He looked back and shrugged. "Once Mary Beth gets an idea in her head, she goes full steam ahead with no time for conversation," he said, shaking his head. "But she'll make a right success of it; you can be sure of that. Will that be cash or charge?"

She handed him her credit card. "Mike. . ." She paused long enough to make him look up with one raised eyebrow. "I wonder if you'd mind letting me have a look through some of your old *Points*." She'd been told he kept them filed in a back room of the store. "I'm doing some research and need to go through some things—oh, back as far as the late eighties."

He narrowed his eyes over the spectacles he hadn't yet removed. "Looking for your mystery boy?"

She nodded.

"Things are a bit of a mess back there, but go ahead. I haven't had time to do much with the old files."

"Thanks," Annie said. "I promise I won't get in your way. You'll never know I'm here."

"No problem." He gestured to the rolls of screening propped up by the counter. "You want me to put this stuff in your car?"

"Never mind. I had to park on the back forty. I'll get it on my way out."

He gave her a brief nod and she followed him through a pine-paneled door and into a room filled with boxes, assorted shelving, and equipment. Along the back wall were metal file cabinets also piled high with stuff. She felt a sneeze coming on even before she was two steps inside.

"It's a bit stuffy," Mike said in gross understatement. "You can open that window over there if you have a mind to." And he left, closing the door behind him.

Where to start? Regretting her choice of white pants, Annie headed for the metal files. She began at the far end, hoping to find a logical order to the stored newspapers, but her hopes were soon dashed. Recent *Points* were printed in color on 11-by-17-inch sheets and folded in half. Most were just one or two folded sheets, but a few issues deemed

particularly newsworthy comprised as many as six folded
sheets.

The Cultural Center's megaprinter did a pretty good job.
Photos were sharp and the text readable. Ian's face showed
up often. He might be dedicating a new wing of the local
library or introducing a new member of the town council.
Reverend Wallace's column contained a short homily under
the heading "Wit and Wisdom."

Earlier editions had been printed in black and white—
sometimes just one sheet printed back to back like a company newsletter. Sometimes the copies were dense with ink
or so light as to be barely legible. They were stacked inside
drawers stuffed so full that the paper was crumpled or torn.
She rifled through them, checking for dates and skimming
over wedding announcements, obituaries, society news, and
local commentary on world events.

"Morgue" was a good name for this place, Annie thought.
The air was as dead as the old news inside. She paused at
the window to breathe. Sweating in her sleeveless tank, she
continued looking for the face of the boy to whom she'd
made a promise.

She found a few issues dating to the seventies and in
the back of the same drawer a short stack from the eighties.
She cleared one end of a cluttered table to spread the copies
out and settled herself precariously on a broken stool near
the window.

She waded through news from villages up and down the
coast. Most related to fishing or tourism, and a few more
intriguing stories were distilled from the Portland articles.
She found everything from disputes over lobster territory to

armed robbery. A July 1986 issue covered the disappearance of a local businessman charged with embezzlement. The kidnapping of a wealthy Portland girl took up a full column in a 1987 issue.

She skipped over fall, winter, and spring issues; the photos of the young boy in her album had been taken in full summer when the beach was crowded. So she scanned items such as July Fourth observances and 4-H fairs, even company picnics and clam bakes. She might look forever and find nothing, of course. The boy was no one special; no one anyone knew. A lost face in the crowd.

Nothing turned up in June or July 1989. August was slim, just two pages in narrow-column format. There were few pictures. She groaned and began skimming the stories: A nor'easter that knocked out power in Stony Point for thirty-six hours, a melee in a downtown Portland bar, an island ferry mishap with three people drowned. One was a Stony Point resident. The ferry mishap story filled most of page two except for a three-inch spot at the far right. And then, when she came to it, every little hair on the back of her neck quivered:

> *August 12, 1989: The body of a young man was found drifting in Casco Bay 30 miles from the city of Portland. His father, an itinerant gardener who had worked in Portland and the villages of Hanover and Stony Point, identified him as sixteen-year-old Cagney Torrez. Cause of death is unknown though believed to be blunt force trauma. Stony Point officials could not comment on information that the boy might be tied to a ring of hotel thieves operating out of Portland.*

She stared at the tiny photo at the left of the notice and knew—as sure as she knew the sun rises in the east—who the boy was. She was carrying his picture in her purse. And now she knew his name.

Decades ago Cagney Torrez had looked out over Stony Point Harbor, watched fishing boats come and go; perhaps he helped his father prune the bushes in Stony Point gardens. He had walked the crowded beach where townies and summer people played in the wind and surf. Then he was dead. Three inches in a dusty newspaper contained his epitaph.

She swallowed, as much from amazement as sorrow, and tucked the paper under her arm with trembling fingers. She gathered her purse, put the stool back in the corner, and left the morgue.

Mike was helping customers when she came out into the store. She wouldn't bother him now, and she was too upset to wait. She'd make a copy and return his original later.

She walked to her car, hardly aware of the fresh air filling her lungs or the sun filtering through lush green trees. She walked down streets alive with the usual sights of an early-summer day in Stony Point. Shoppers peered in windows, senior citizens licked ice cream cones. These were sights Cagney Torrez must have seen all those years ago when he was a boy. Sights he'd never see again. He never had a chance to grow up, to marry or have children, or to make a place for himself in the world. It was just so wrong. How had it happened? In her mind's eye, she pictured him floating in the bay. What had he thought about before the water began to fill his lungs?

"Hey, wait! Don't you want your stuff?" Mike Malone was sprinting toward her, laden with rolls of screening.

"Oh! I can't believe I forgot. I'm so sorry." She popped the trunk lid so he could deposit her purchases.

"You find what you were looking for?"

"I think so," she said softly. "I'm afraid the boy in the photo is dead."

Mike closed the trunk and stood looking at her, his brown eyes a study in dismay. "That's terrible. How did it happen?"

"I don't know." She held the paper out to him, waited while he pulled his glasses from his shirt pocket. He scanned the article and handed it back without a word. He shook his head sadly.

"Mind if I make a copy and get this back to the morgue later?" She wasn't sure what she would do with it, but she owed it to this poor boy to make some kind of memorial, if only to preserve the notice of his death.

"No problem, Annie. Sorry your quest didn't turn out better."

"I almost wish I hadn't taken it on. I had so hoped. . ." She let the words fall away. She didn't know what she had wished, but certainly not this.

She drove away, pondering the small sad face etched in her mind. Perhaps she owed him more than just preserving the article. His story should be known. His life had been cut short; someone should know why.

─9─

"Wait! Don't jump!" Annie screamed into the raging wind.

The boy stood on the lighthouse's high rocky ledge, wind whipping his dark jeans. Hands in his pockets, he stared into the roiling surf that crashed against the jagged boulders. Waves rolled over him until his body shone in the moonlight. Shoulders hunched, he straddled the rocks in bare brown feet.

"No!" The wind howled around her ears, swallowed the sound, and pushed it back into her throat. He was so small, so far away. Why couldn't she run faster? She raced toward him, arms wildly waving. (Didn't they say that was precisely the wrong thing to do? Startle a person on the precipice of death?) Still, she ran on.

Suddenly he turned toward her, and she saw his face clearly, though they were more than a hundred yards apart. Enormous haunting eyes fixed in fear or longing looked out of a beautiful face surrounded by wild black hair.

She tried to run, but the wind blew with brutal force, holding her back. Her feet were iron clods. "Cagney!" she called.

His hands came out of his pockets. One arm coiled toward her, the fingers splayed, pleading. His mouth opened in something like a smile or terrible acquiescence.

"I'm coming! Wait!"

He spun around as though startled. Had she come too close? "No-o-o-o-o!" she screamed. Even as her plea came back into her ears, she saw him fall—neatly, gently—a perfect tuck and roll. A mighty crash of thunderous waves and then silence.

Annie woke with a start in Grey Gables' high east bedroom, her body covered with sweat, and she was freezing.

It had been a long time since she'd had a nightmare. When her mother died of tuberculosis contracted on a mission trip to Africa, she had dreamed. Terrible dreams. Not long after, her father died of a stroke. Except for her dear grandmother, she might never have gotten over the tragedy of losing her parents. When she wakened in the night in this very bedroom, Gram's touch had been a soothing balm, her voice a lullaby. Her parents had died loving what they'd committed their lives to, she said. Judy and George Spencer had flown back to the loving hands that created them. They were safe. Nor had their short journey been in vain; their work lived on in the hearts they touched. Tears preserved in a bottle—too precious to waste?

Annie pushed the covers back, struggled into her favorite blue silk robe and went downstairs. She definitely needed coffee. Boots met her halfway up, curled around her ankles, and looked up at her inquisitively. Can a cat have a concerned look on its whiskery face?

At the kitchen table, Annie pulled Boots up onto her lap, stroked her warm fur. She'd been sitting in her favorite place on the window ledge, where the morning sun beamed in like a great radiator. As she soaked up the same healing sun, Annie felt almost euphoric. However bad life might be at times, it was far preferable to the world of dream.

Of course she knew where last night's terror had started: in the stuffy back room at Malone's after reading about Cagney Torrez, about his body found floating in the bay. If only she could go back to the days when there was hope that he might still be alive walking around Stony Point whole and well. But he was dead.

He'd been little more than a child and she totally oblivious to him. By then she'd graduated from Texas A&M two thousand miles away and was no longer spending summers with Gram. She'd been busy loving life and Wayne; Cagney Torrez had. . . well, what *had* been going on in his young life? What terrors had he known?

"Blunt force trauma," the news report claimed. Either he had bashed his own head on the rocks or someone had killed him. And it might well have happened somewhere near the friendly little village of Stony Point that had been her haven for so many summers as a lonely child. It had not protected this boy. Who was he really? He was the son of a gardener said to have worked in Stony Point, among other places along the coast. But what were Cagney Torrez's hopes and dreams? And who had put an end to them, if not Cagney himself?

"I don't know, Boots," she said softly as she stroked the silken ears. "This is one sad treasure in Gram's attic. Maybe we should have let sleeping dogs lie."

Boots looked up suddenly, the tip of her tail curling ever so slightly.

"Sorry," she said, grinning at her metaphor. She sighed.

"Well, dogs and cats aside, work eases a troubled mind. It's back to the screens again this morning."

Boots jumped off her lap, as though she could actually understand, and went to the door. But Annie still had to get dressed and prepare for the grueling task she'd failed at so miserably before. This time she was armed with sawhorses and clamps and a set of instructions from the Internet.

Perhaps she'd forgo a shower. It would be a waste of time, no doubt, since she'd need another after fighting with the screens. But she washed her face and neck vigorously, eager to wash away the night with its frightening dreams. She sprayed on a little perfume before vigorously brushing her hair. She pulled on jeans and an old college T-shirt and planned to be invisible if anyone came to call.

A light rain overnight had left the garden sparkling. The rose bushes rambling along the porch rail glistened, their small pink petals wide to the morning sun. Heavy peony heads bowed to the earth as if in prayer or surrender, but they too would perk up once the sun dried their tears.

She walked around to the back of the house, keeping to the flagstones lest her feet get drenched in wet grass. The woods beyond lay thick and shady in a thousand green hues from chartreuse to nearly black. They could be formidable on a dark night.

She loaded the supplies from Malone's into Gram's old wheelbarrow and heisted them up to the porch. She caressed the wheelbarrow's sun-faded handle. She remembered actually being small enough to ride in that wheelbarrow. Gram would lift her inside, place gardening tools in her lap, and off they would go for a morning of weeding, planting, and trimming.

When the sun began to penetrate their light clothing and leave them wilting, she and Gram would stop to rest beneath the willow at the edge of the creek. Cattails and reeds waved gently beneath the sweeping branches, their slender leaves shining silvery in the yellow light. They'd munch crisp, green apples before returning to work.

The memories were everywhere; how Gram had loved this place. Annie sighed as she selected the first of the screens for repair. Maybe it would be wise to speed up the sprucing and sorting process before Grey Gables took too firm a hold on her.

She removed the damaged material from the first of the frames and rolled out a length of new screening. Boots, having learned that screens and sharp feline claws did not mix well, contented herself to sit and watch. But suddenly she sprang up from the porch rail where she'd been sunning and dropped down into the bushes below.

At the same moment, Dorian Jones in casual jeans and a sky-blue polo shirt came up the path.

Annie heard her own sharp intake of breath and looked down in dismay at her faded shirt and grungy jeans. All hope of invisibility was shattered. Dorian Jones was not simply passing by; he was coming up the winding path from the street directly to Grey Gables.

The screen she'd been working on fell off the sawhorse, followed by the hammer, which dropped smack into the middle of it. "Oh!" she groaned.

"Who's winning? You or the screens?" he asked, cocking his head to one side. The sun shone on his short-cropped hair, turning it golden. His unusual eyes held mild amusement. Perhaps he had a sense of humor, after all.

"Trying to," she said dismally, brushing off the front of her jeans and tugging down her baggy Texas A&M shirt. "I'm afraid I'm having a bit of trouble with these old screens. But I'm keeping Malone's Hardware in business."

"Can I help?" he inquired, perching a foot on the bottom porch step and pausing there.

Canvas Gucci loafers, if she wasn't mistaken. Over two hundred dollars a pair. The Ralph Lauren polo looked as if it had just come off the rack.

"I'd really like to help. It would give me a chance to give something back after all your grandmother did for me. It would also please me to be of service to her lovely granddaughter."

"Oh, but you're on vacation. I couldn't possibly ask you. . ."

"But you're not asking; I'm offering." He smiled, revealing even, white teeth. "And besides, I've had plenty of time to walk the beach and explore your quaint shops and restaurants. It would give me pleasure to help restore a beautiful place like Grey Gables." His gaze swept slowly, almost reverently, over the house and came back to rest on her face.

"I'd be crazy to refuse," she said, and stepped back to reveal her dubious handiwork. "Wally Carson usually does this sort of thing for me, but he's laid up with a broken arm. I have a feeling he probably could do better with one arm in a sling than I'm doing with two."

At that, he stepped lightly onto the porch, pushing up his sleeves and effectively showing off those incredible biceps she had noticed the first time she'd seen him. He quickly surveyed the disordered scene, moved the sawhorses closer together, and set up a torn screen. His fingers moved deftly over the wooden frames. Sturdy fingers, smooth knuckles, and—she found herself checking—no ring on the left hand.

She watched awhile in silence and then declared, "I'll go make us some iced tea." When she stepped around him to go into the house, she smelled his cologne: a mix of ocean and pine. Wild, woodsy, and oddly alluring.

Wayne, a Texan through and through, hadn't worn cologne. But this heady fragrance stirred something almost primitive and frightened her a little.

She went inside to prepare the tea, grateful for an opportunity to collect her scattered wits and to run a brush through her hair. It had been quite a while since she felt like this, all fluttery and on tiptoe, like a teenager on her first date. Yet as she passed the hall mirror, she rebuked herself sternly. Loneliness was part of the human condition, after all. Everyone had to deal with it. It was wise to do so carefully. *You know virtually nothing about the man on your porch*, an inner voice said.

Loneliness is a stalker, she knew, with no laws to circumvent its crimes. You could go about your business in an orderly, usual manner, carry out the obligations that mark your life. Then without warning it could strike—maybe in the form of a lone sparrow shaped like a dawn-gray teardrop landing on your windowsill. Its questing eye peers into your soul, and you're one with it, bewildered and alone.

She set tall glasses on Gram's best wooden tray and went back outside. Dorian had finished two of the screens, which were now taut and straight, the corners perfectly angled.

"That's amazing!" she said, surveying his work. "I could have slaved all morning, and they'd never look like that. I guess you really *are* good with your hands."

He shrugged and set the screens upright against the side of the porch. "I'll help you get them back in."

She led him to each of the windows in question, where he installed the screens, complete with the rubber stripping Mike had thrown in with her other supplies. She'd had no clue how that worked, but Dorian affixed it with ease.

They were largely quiet while they worked on the remaining screens, the hum of bees and twitter of birds for accompaniment. Annie felt a strange sense of pleasure in the simple homey tasks and could almost wish to stop time, to keep this remarkable flush of youth and wonder.

"I'd like to help you with other things," he said as they cleaned up the work area and put tools away.

"Oh, I couldn't ask that of you. . ." But once again he assured her that she hadn't asked, that he had offered and that he would welcome the chance to talk and share memories of Stony Point and her grandmother.

"I'd be happy to strip that down and refinish it for you," he said, gesturing to the gateleg table set out at the far end of the porch. Before he'd broken his arm, Wally had purchased refinishing supplies. They were stacked on a tarp spread beneath the table to protect the floor. "I have a few business appointments in the area, but I still have plenty of time," he continued. "I'd like nothing better than to work with that beautiful wood."

"Really?" she said, realizing she had been mourning the finished screens.

"If you just leave it out, I'll come by and work on it when I can. Think of me as Wally in disguise."

"Only if you'll let me pay you, as I would Wally."

He shrugged. "If you must, but it would be my pleasure..." He paused, looked directly at her before completing his sentence, ". . .and a real pleasure to refinish a fine piece of furniture for a lovely lady."

She felt herself reddening. Clearly he meant to convey that he was interested in more than fine wood. "We haven't had our tea yet," she said nervously, and indicated the round wicker table where she'd left the tray with a clean tea towel spread over it. She pointed to a chair across from her own.

He pulled the chair out to accommodate his long legs, sat down and drank most of the tea in a few quick swallows. When he leaned back, the sun ignited a gold chain around his neck and highlighted dark hairs on his chest. Settling one ankle on his alternate knee, he peered out over the garden as though appraising the view. "So, have you decided yet?"

"Decided what?"

"Whether you're going to stay or sell."

Had they discussed that? Perhaps in an oblique sort of way, yet it took her by surprise. She hesitated, followed his gaze out over the landscape, and then felt his attention return to her. "I want to give it some time," she said. "There are repairs that should be done. And of course Gram left many things behind in this big place, things that should be distributed among her relatives and friends."

He said nothing, but his eyes—those odd mesmerizing eyes—were looking into hers. She shrugged and looked away. "I don't feel any need to hurry. My life has come to a sort of stopping place, anyway." She paused. She hadn't meant to open the door for discussion about her personal life.

He didn't say anything at first, just looked from beneath dark brows that were oddly discordant with his light hair. And Annie recalled Alice's off-hand comment about hair coloring. Men were as vain as women, she supposed, and this one moved in some pretty upscale circles. Perhaps he had a hairdresser.

Dorian traced the rim of his glass thoughtfully. "I must say I'm surprised that someone like you is here alone. I mean, I thought you'd be married or. . ." He let the sentence drift, even as his eyes drifted into space before he continued, and something hard crept into his voice. "Of course, those things do have a way of disintegrating."

"My husband passed away," she said more coldly than she intended to.

"I'm sorry," he said quickly, leaning forward. "I just meant, well, we do tend to transfer our own failures into other people's lives." He paused, holding her gaze. "I was married once. It was a long time ago." He brightened then, obviously dismissing a less-than-pleasant memory that he'd decided wasn't worth his time. He gave her a penetrating and slightly playful glance. "And if I may say so, my lady, no man in his right mind would deliberately give up someone like you unless he had to."

She felt a flush of pleasure, even as the red flags waved furiously in her mind. She poured more tea into his glass and remembered Gram's warning epithet: Flattery is like chewing gum. Chew but don't swallow. "You're very gallant, Mr. Dorian Jones," she said and laughed to cover the effect his words were having on her. Was she blushing?

She busied herself moving items around on the tray. She'd been feeling like a teenager at her first prom instead of a mature woman with a grown child. Get a grip, she told herself for at least the second time in fifteen minutes.

"Tell me," he said, touching his lips to the glass and regarding her slowly. "What sorts of things are you finding in that old attic?"

"What?" The question seemed to come out of the blue. Or had she simply been derailed by his charm and missed something?

"Every old house of this vintage has an attic," he explained reasonably. "Surely that's where your grandmother kept special things to pass on to grandchildren like yours."

"Of course." She swallowed, tucked a small piece of lemon bread into her mouth.

"Well, I'm finding nothing very valuable, except some needlework of Gram's. There was a huge jar of buttons worth about fifty dollars. . .and some old paintings and tapestries, photographs and letters."

She frowned. Cagney Torrez had largely faded from her mind while she'd been with Dorian, and she felt suddenly penitent. "It's fun trying to identify people you knew long ago. Even to find yourself in snapshots." She realized that Dorian had gone quiet again. "Some memories can be troubling too, I suppose," she added.

He stood up with sudden finality and tucked his hands into the pockets of his jeans. "So shall we say tomorrow?" He extracted one hand and looked at his watch. "Oh, no. . . I forgot. I have an appointment tomorrow. Better make it Friday. I can't say what time for sure, but if you leave the table out on the porch, I'll work on it as I can. You don't even need to be here. You can just go on about your usual business."

He stepped off the porch and took a few steps away before turning around. She'd been trying to thank him, to say he needn't amend his schedule for her sake. But he waved his hand to silence her attempts at appreciation. "Thanks for the tea and for a most enjoyable afternoon." And he disappeared down the sloping path, the sun making a halo of his golden head.

~ 10 ~

Wally Carson trudged along the shore, listening to the sound of waves rushing in, scudding around the rocks, and falling back again. The steady rhythm comforted him. It was timeless and predictable—unlike so much in his life right now.

He'd left the cottage early to make his way to the harbor. The sun hadn't yet warmed the sand, and the cold morning dampness soaked into his sandaled feet. He shivered and hunched his shoulders, seeking more warmth from his old hooded sweatshirt than it was capable of giving. The movement sparked a twinge in his left arm still encased in its heavy cast. *What kind of an idiot falls out of a tree?* he rebuked himself.

"Blasted car won't turn over," he had raved moments ago when he stormed back into the kitchen of the tiny cottage that leaked like a sieve when it rained. Peggy stirred oatmeal, and six-year-old Emily was tying a towel around the neck of her favorite doll, a cloth ballerina with a little short skirt. She had pink satin slippers with ribbons criss-crossing up her fat ankles.

"Madeline, you have to eat all your oatmeal so you have energy for your exercises," she had told it, wagging her finger in its flat, mask-like face.

Wally groaned, remembering the scene. Why couldn't

anything go right? Between his private contracting as a handyman and Peggy's tips from the Cup and Saucer, they had squirreled away a little money. Emily would finally get the ballet lessons she wanted so much, and they could get the new roof on the cottage before winter. Then the recession had hit, sending everyone scrambling to make ends meet. Building projects had come to a halt; even repair jobs had fallen off—except for a few like Grey Gables. Annie Dawson had hired him to work on the old place, and things were going well. Then the stupid fall at the Hodges place, and here he was back to square one.

Peggy had been a rock through it all, though he'd seen the disappointment in her round blue eyes. "Never mind," she'd told him sweetly when he'd cursed his rattletrap old car that morning. "Emily and I can ride with Jane Swenson." Jane ran the Dress to Impress shop in town and didn't live too far from them. And he could walk the two miles to the waterfront. It wouldn't kill him. Besides, it would give him time to think.

Two steps forward. Three steps back. He was getting older and what did he have to show for it? A drafty cottage and a part-time job cleaning the dock and locking up the fish house after all the traps were unloaded. And if it weren't for Annie and Ian Butler, he wouldn't have even that.

Whoosh-sh-sh, whoosh-sh-sh. The shushing sounds of the water echoed his frustration. He shoved his good hand into his pocket. Of course, he knew he'd been lucky in landing Peggy, who lived next door to the Carsons. Ten years ago his life had been headed nowhere but down. Like his father and his brother, he'd been living fast and hard. He'd gotten into one scrape after another.

They were three men with no feminine hand to gentle their rough edges. His mother died when he was seven. That's when the downward spiral had begun for his father. Dad had spent his days fishing from his boat, a sixteen-foot Swampscott Dory, and too many nights carousing with his mates. Wally picked up a small round stone and threw it hard into the bay. The dory might have been his one day if Dad hadn't cracked her up along Camberwell Island's jagged coast.

After Dad died of a stroke, Wally and Jem were left to their own teenage devices. Jeremiah and Wallace Henry Carson. Had it been his mom's idea or his dad's to give him the name of the thirty-third vice president of the United States? The name was turned backward of course, and he supposed that was fitting. He sent a second stone flying and frowned when it barely cleared the shoreline.

He and Peg had gone to school together, but when he'd quit at sixteen, she'd given up on him. Started hanging out with that creepy Neal Sorenson. It nearly killed him to see his beautiful Peggy pawed by that Ivy Leaguer who thought he was God's gift to the world.

Wally put the hood up over his head as a gust of wind blew across the headland. Why was he rehashing old history? But some memories were pretty good. Twelve years ago he had crashed Jem's old Chrysler and landed in the hospital with a concussion and a broken leg. Peg was a hospital aide in those days and somewhere during her 4 P.M. to midnight shift, she'd fallen in love with him again. He'd have cracked up sooner if he'd known.

Not that it was all smooth sailing from then on, especially when after five years of trying, there was no baby. Peggy's fondest dream was for a child. She even cried herself to sleep sometimes wanting it. Just when he thought he'd been cursed because he couldn't give her a child, she discovered she was pregnant on the eve of her twenty-ninth birthday.

That was some celebration they had. They cooked burgers on the grill and invited half the town to a rip-roaring party. Who would have believed dumb old Wally could land the prettiest girl in Stony Point and get the second prettiest in his daughter, Emily Sue Carson, future ballerina and prima donna of the world?

"You're not dumb, and I'm going to tie your ears in a knot if you don't stop putting yourself down!" Peggy would reach up with those quick little arms of hers and wrap them around his neck. Instead of whopping him one like she promised, she'd kiss him hard and deep. When she did that, he thought he'd die of some kind of wonder.

But the truth was, he'd never read a book all the way through in his whole life, and sometimes he was hard-pressed to read the directions on a prefab workbench or a knocked-down cabinet from a discount store. Some comedown for Peggy: from college boy Neal Sorenson to dumb old Wally. If he could only make good, bring in enough money to end their worries, at least for a little while. Maybe he could win the lottery. But Peggy would kill him if she thought he spent money buying numbers that were what, five million to one? With his luck, they could be fifteen to one and he'd still not come close.

But a guy could dream. Think what he could do with that kind of money. He'd use some of it to buy that thirty-foot aluminum Kingfisher with its 150-gallon cockpit and fishbox. He could run a string of fifty traps or more. Peggy and Emily wouldn't have to scrimp for the things they wanted.

"Dream on, dolt," he told himself.

In his mind's eye he could see Peggy giving him that look. She was always reminding him not to put himself down, that there were plenty of people in the world who would do that for him. But he'd taken a good look at himself, and he hadn't seen anything to set the world on fire. He didn't even have a decent job. And he wanted so much for Peggy and Emily. A guy had to think about things like paying for college and a nice wedding some day. Wally shivered as he took a long look into the future, a future that seemed pretty bleak to him.

He liked walking the beach when it was all but deserted. Near the point, it narrowed, and spruces lining the cliffs pierced the sky with their raggedy tops. The world rolled on year after year—sea, sky, land—as it had for hundreds of years. People came and went and were forgotten. A sobering sense of loss blew through him like a blast of wind through a tunnel.

"You're a lucky young man," Reverend Wallace had told him when he'd survived that crash. Peggy told him later he'd come real close to entering the pearly gates. "The good Lord's not finished with you yet." Wally grimaced. He liked the silver-haired minister, but he couldn't figure out the good Lord's plan—if such a thing existed.

"When they put you in the ground, that's all there is." He could hear his dad saying. "The only slice of pie you're gonna get is down here, boy." He didn't remember much his father ever said. Most of what he could recall had been mumbled over a glass of Jack Daniels.

He peered up at the sky where pink and orange ribbons trailed like the slipper strings of Emily's ballerina doll. The trees jutting out of craggy rocks were silhouetted against the colorful background. What was the point of it all? There was something huge out there, something waiting, hovering on the horizon, but how did you find your place in it? Was there a God out there who really cared about him—and Peggy and Emily?

Wally sensed rather than heard that he wasn't alone on the beach after all. He turned to see a well-built man striding loosely but purposefully in khaki pants and green shirt, a dark jacket slung over his shoulder. He lifted a hand in greeting, quickened his pace. "Morning," he called and fell in step beside Wally.

"Back at ya," Wally said affably. The guy was a good head taller than he was and could have posed for one of those muscle-building ads, maybe even for a line of men's grooming products. He was one of those golden boys. Even his hair was trimmed neatly around perfectly shaped ears. Wally felt a familiar stab of inferiority.

"You must be Wally," the man said, smiling and putting out a hand. "Dorian Jones. Beach is beautiful this time of day." He raised his head and inhaled deeply. "A walk in the early morning gives a man heart for a good day's work, doesn't it?"

The friendly manner cheered Wally, and he liked being addressed by name. He peered up into the handsome face. He was a little older than Wally had first thought, probably about the same age he was.

"You're Annie's friend. The one. . ." But he broke off. He'd heard Annie Dawson had someone doing *his* job.

"Yes. I'm not the carpenter you are, but I've been trying to help her out. Sorry about your arm." Unusual eyes, tinged yellow, roamed over Wally's cast.

Wally felt a swelling in his chest. He shrugged, trying not to show that the compliment had pleased him. "You're. . .uh. . .vacationing around Stony Point?"

"And quite a place it is," Dorian said. "There's nothing like a good sandy beach and the peace of a friendly village. It sure beats the grind and grime of the city."

"You're from New York, right?" Wally had heard that the handsome summer visitor was some kind of antique dealer. Jewelry, mostly. From the look of him he'd made good too. Had the smell of money and success all over him. Peggy had told him some high muck-a-muck from New York was going to be judge and auctioneer at the gig Mary Beth was planning. Peggy was planning to enter Emily's Disney princess quilt and was working like mad to finish it.

"I get around a lot in my business, but you're right. Most recently, I'm from the Big Apple."

They walked several paces in silence, Wally wondering what to say that wouldn't make him sound dumb.

"And what about you? I understand you're working down at the wharf."

"Yeah, just helping out while the arm's healing, you

know," Wally said. "I hose down the dock, keep an eye out for the boats. Stuff like that."

"I guess they depend on you to close up after all the boats are in." His words were tinged with admiration. "I expect that's pretty important." He nodded decisively and then continued, "I've always been fascinated by fishing, especially lobstering. How do you get those delicious little suckers in those traps?"

"Well, it's no big deal," Wally said. Was this overkill on the flattery or what?

They were nearing the point where the beach ended; the coast grew rocky and primitive. A miniforest, mostly spruce and scrub pine, shadowed the old lighthouse beyond. His companion stopped, scanned the scene with those odd yellowish eyes, and turned to Wally. "That scene is just like a postcard. Unforgettable."

Wally shrugged. "Guess I never think about it. See it every day."

"Yes, I suppose you do," he said thoughtfully. Then, as though something had just occurred to him, he said, "I wonder if you'd consider doing a little errand for me."

Ah, there it was, what all the buttering up was about.

"Oh, I'll make it worth your time. A good man is worth his hire."

Wally pondered briefly how the wealthy tourist came to a conclusion about his character. Perhaps Annie had put in a good word for him. She'd been kind to him and Peggy. He waited, his right foot propped up on a flat rock.

"I collect and appraise antique items, so I'm often called on for professional advice," Dorian said. "My contacts

always know how to find me, even when I'm on vacation."
He tapped a cell phone affixed to the belt at his hip. "I'm
expecting a package. A small but very valuable package.
It'll be coming in by boat—a small fishing craft. I'm going
to be away until tomorrow, and I need someone to pick it
up for me."

Wally shrugged. "Suppose I could."

Dorian had pulled out his wallet and was shuffling
through an array of crisp bills. He stopped, pulled out two
hundred-dollar bills and folded them inside his large fist.
His voice took on a hushed, conspiratorial tone, and he
peered closely into Wally's face. "The package is from an
insurance company working on behalf of a high-level client.
It's strictly confidential. I'd like you to pick it up for me and
hold onto it until I get back."

Wally felt his mouth go dry. Two hundred dollars to pick
up a package? "How. . .how will I know?" he stammered.
"When. . ."

"It'll arrive later this afternoon, and my client will find
you. The package will be inside an ordinary lobster trap.
Ingenious, huh?" He smiled broadly. "He'll ask you to deliver
it to Mr. Dorian Jones. You'll extract the package—it'll fit in
your pocket—and hold onto it for me. You'll meet me out
there." He pointed up to Butler's Lighthouse. "Tomorrow
night at ten o'clock sharp. Right?"

Consternation had to be written all over his face, because
Dorian grinned and spread his hands in an apologetic
gesture. "Sorry for all the intrigue, Wally, but it's important
to my client that the shipment be completely protected and
anonymous." He opened his hand and extended the folded

bills. "Can I count on you?"

Wally stared at the money. It was the strangest offer he'd ever received. He didn't make two hundred dollars in a week helping Todd Butler, and all he had to do for this rich tourist was deliver a package.

"Annie says you can be trusted. So I'm trusting you," he said. With that he clapped Wally on his good shoulder and gave it a reassuring squeeze. "I have to pick up a rental car, but I'll be back tomorrow like I said. Ten o'clock at the lighthouse."

Wally drew himself up to his full height, which wasn't enough to look Jones in the eye. "I'll be there," he said. They shook hands, and Dorian Jones made off toward the cliff road that led back to town. Wally stared after him, stunned by his good fortune. They'd have the money for Emily's lessons much sooner than he'd hoped. Peggy would be so proud.

The tall stranger turned back. "But remember, not a word to anyone. Not your friends or Annie and not even that sweet Peggy of yours."

Wally nodded and watched Dorian Jones stride across the rocky expanse.

Overhead, two gulls circled and screamed in the brightening sky. Wally stuffed the bills into his back pocket and secured the button on the flap with shaky fingers. It could be the excitement of earning the fastest two hundred bucks he'd made in years or a niggling concern about the way Jones had said "that sweet Peggy of yours" like it was some kind of warning.

How did he know his wife's name, anyway? He bit

the inside of each cheek. The guy was tight with Annie; she must have mentioned Peggy. As for the big bills, well, rich guys like him threw around money like that without batting an eye.

People were funny. Once he'd sold half a dozen lobsters off the back of his dad's boat to a guy from Jersey for fifty bucks. He might even have paid more to entertain the fancy guests who'd arrived without warning. But that was in his wild-oats youth before Peggy had got hold of him.

He'd surprise her with the extra money. Maybe they'd make a night of it, the three of them, and go somewhere besides the Cup and Saucer for a good supper. Wally headed toward the harbor, where the fishermen were already setting out with their traps and gear, and wished the afternoon's errand was over.

～ 11 ～

*I*an ducked into the Cup and Saucer and headed for his usual booth in the center of the café. He liked the comforting aroma of coffee and bacon and the mix of other smells that gave it its distinctive ambience. He liked it much better since they'd gone smoke-free, but even back in the old days, the Cup and Saucer had felt like home.

"Morning, Ira. Tim." He waved with his usual ardor, glad to see old friends. A few new folks breakfasted as well, this being the beginning of the summer season when the streets of Stony Point burgeoned with tourists. He nodded and smiled at them and slid into his booth, feeling uncharacteristically tired.

Peggy set a plate of pancakes on the counter in front of Ira Heath and headed toward Ian's booth, eyes bright as blueberries wet with rain. Her dark hair stood up in a series of short spikes, and two longer strands dripped down at her ears. Her beautician sister had been at it again.

"Morning, Mr. Mayor," Peggy said, her quick smile spilling over him. She always called him that, never Ian, and he'd come to wait for that charming greeting from the effervescent Peggy.

"You're looking bright-eyed and bushy-tailed this morning," he told her.

"Ugh!" she chirped. "Do I look like a squirrel?"

"Just an expression to say you're looking well." Which she knew, of course, but Peggy liked to tease him almost as much as he enjoyed teasing her. He was glad to see her looking so happy. No doubt Emily had a lot to do with that. She and Wally doted on that child. They'd waited so long for her. If anything happened to her. . .but he wouldn't even finish that thought.

"I know your 'usual' order. But let me try to tempt you away from it. . .We've got cinnamon pancakes this morning," Peggy said, "and Marie's special eggs Benedict and sausage links." This morning her nails were bright green with tiny white daisies painted on them. She was a walking summer meadow; Mitzy had struck again!

He put up a hand as though to ward off a cholesterol attack. "I'll take the special eggs, with wheat toast of course. But skip the sausages."

"Coming up," she said and twirled her chubby self around. She still looked like a high school cheerleader. He was glad he'd talked Todd into giving Wally a job down at the dock.

He looked around at the simple booths with their smooth seats of dark green vinyl. Real ivy trailed from enormous pots shaped like cups, perched on high shelves around the café. Blinds at the windows tempered the morning sun, and green-and-white checkered valances gave the place a homey atmosphere. Napkins were couched appropriately in the center of large yellow cups set in yellow saucers, with pig or cow-shaped salt-and-pepper shakers fitting nicely at the side.

The town had a lot of pride, and he was proud of it

too. They'd been through hard times; even now with the economic downturn, it hadn't been easy, but they'd all pulled together. He took a drink of the coffee and ignored the county newspaper Peggy had brought with the coffee. He didn't feel like reading it this morning; likely there would be reports of thefts and domestic disturbances. He wasn't ready for the *Wall Street Journal*, either, which surprisingly he'd left at home this morning. He'd spied the latest edition of *The Point,* though, when he'd come in. A small stack lay on the table by the front door for visitors to take as they came and went. He had picked one up and quickly saw the ad for the needlework fair.

At that moment, Mary Beth breezed in and came toward him, her sensible shoes making little tapping sounds on the faux stone floor. She was dressed in dark slacks and a flowered blouse, overlaid with her trademark smock. Her short gray curls appeared slightly damp and clung neatly around her face. Without makeup she still sported a healthy glow. Her best feature, he thought as she approached, were intelligent eyes beneath naturally arched brows.

"Good morning, Ian. Mind if I join you for a quick cup?"

He rose, waited for her to seat herself before sitting down again. "Morning, Mary Beth. You're looking well." And she was, but he hadn't missed the light shadows beneath her eyes. A bit of overwork and worry over her ailing mother, no doubt. "How is your mother doing?"

He knew there had been trying days when Mary Beth had to rush off to Seaside Hills to calm a less-than-sober-minded parent. Once he'd driven her there himself when word came that Mrs. Brock had wandered into the laundry room, climbed into a utility closet, and refused to come out. That had been a year ago or more, he thought now.

"Mother's holding her own. She stays in bed much more than she used to." Mary Beth paused, a shadow crossing her face. "There were times when I wished for that, but. . ." She broke off, drew in her breath. "She needs more oxygen these days to keep her comfortable." A slight smile lit her eyes. "We had a good visit yesterday. She. . .well. . .she knew who I was and she. . ." But Mary Beth let the words die away and sipped her coffee in silence.

"I'm sorry," Ian said gently. "There's nothing harder than watching a loved one change before your eyes." He dismissed a vision of Arianna that suddenly passed before him, reviving an ache in the middle of his chest somewhere.

Focusing on Mary Beth instead, he remembered that things had not always been good between mother and daughter. He'd been surprised when Beatrice Bennington Brock had agreed to come to Stony Point, a place she'd had no apparent appreciation for in years past. Nor had Melanie, Mary Beth's sister, come around more than once or twice a year, if that. He wondered if Mary Beth missed her. Likely not as much as she missed Melanie's daughter, Amy. She was the light of Mary Beth's life, along with her shop and needlework club.

The girl—well, she'd be a woman well into her thirties now. A shy, quiet person, Ian recalled, preferring to stay at the cottage with Mary Beth or take long walks along the ocean.

"Seen much of that niece of yours lately?" he asked quietly.

Mary Beth gnawed briefly at the inside of her cheek. "Not for two years," she said and paused to sip her coffee. The shadow in her eyes deepened. "I phoned her about her grandma. My mother always was a difficult woman, but Amy loved her; news of her failing health was hard for her to hear. Of course, Mother's mind hasn't been right for some time. . ."

Ian put a comforting hand on Mary Beth's, patted it briefly, and withdrew it. He knew how she felt. His uncle had suffered from Alzheimer's. A brilliant chemist who could track the most difficult sums and calculate complicated equations had gradually lost the ability to remember the way to his own bedroom.

Mary Beth looked up, squared her jaw. "Well, the Lord doesn't put more on us than we can stand. Reverend Wallace always says so. And I guess it's good to believe it. Besides. . ." She gave him a rueful smile. ". . .there's far too much to do to dwell on trouble, I always say." She shook her head, effectively dismissing negative conversation. "Now, is everything okay for the tenth of August?"

"The council gave it thumbs up. How is it going?"

"The Hook and Needle ladies are working hard, Ian. Bless them. And Annie's going to donate a Betsy Original to be auctioned off. Folks are offering donations and getting excited about it. The best news is we've found a real expert to judge the contest and to be our auctioneer." Mary Beth's eyes grew brighter than he'd seen them since she sat down.

"That was lucky. Who's the expert judge?"

"Well, believe it or not, he's a Mr. Dorian Jones, a much sought-after expert in all sorts of antiques. He's a trained gemologist, so our Annie says. And he has connections with some of the best auction houses in the country, even Christie's and Sotheby's." She intoned the two famous names in a reverential whisper.

"You don't say," Ian said, studying Mary Beth's animated face. "Our Annie is a source of all kinds of curiosities. And apparently she's not keeping them all in the attic." He had teased her about attic curiosities just the other day when they met on the street. She'd given back as good as she got, and he'd come to depend on her for that. She'd really brightened things up since she'd come to Stony Point. She'd become a trusted friend and entered into the life of the community with uncommon zest.

"So who is this expert?" he asked, trying to recall new-comers in the village. There were too many to keep track of, and that sometimes unnerved him.

"Name's Dorian Jones. He once worked for Betsy Holden years ago. Annie says he was just a boy then, working to earn money for college. Did odd jobs for Betsy, repairing and refinishing furniture and such. He claims Betsy is the one who fostered his love of antiques, got him into his vocation. He's been helping Annie out at Grey Gables now that Wally's laid up. Says it's a way of giving back for what Annie's grandmother did for him."

A picture formed in Ian's mind. A handsome man in his late forties, dark blond hair, disgustingly fit. Yes, he'd seen him at Annie's once when he'd driven by to enlist her help with the Mothers' March of Dimes campaign. But he hadn't seen him around town much. No doubt he wasn't into shopping at boutiques or sunbathing on the beach. He hoped Annie wasn't getting in over her head. But she was a pretty level-headed woman. She could take care of herself. Still, he found himself wondering just who this Mr. Jones was.

"Well, I have a big day ahead. The tourists will be swarming. And I'm expecting a shipment of yarn today, too." Mary Beth rose and pulled her wallet from her pants pocket.

"I'll get it, Mary Beth. You go on," Ian said, getting up. He stood to the side as she climbed out of the booth.

"Ian, you're a prince. Thanks!" And she was off, her sturdy bulk marking a quick path to the Cup and Saucer's door.

He settled back in the seat. He'd eaten only one piece of the toast and wondered where his appetite was this morning. He sometimes made eggs or oatmeal at home but had been too fidgety to remain in his own comfortable kitchen. Comfortable but often lonely, he had to admit.

Getting used to being a bachelor again had taken some doing—even with the addition of Tartan, a standard Schnauzer who had its origins in the old herding and guard breeds of Europe. Robust, medium-sized, and with an aristocratic bearing, the standard Schnauzer was a popular subject of such painters as Sir Joshua Reynolds and Rembrandt.

Arianna had preferred their Yorkie, Yolanda, but she had become ill and had to be put to sleep in her sixth year of life. So here it was, Ian realized, the source of his unsettledness today. Arianna's fiftieth birthday. He hadn't even realized it until now. There would be no party with her favorite German chocolate cake and no celebrating, unless heaven included such things.

It had happened quickly. Who could have predicted that her headaches were symptoms of a brain aneurysm? When it ruptured, endovascular coiling was performed within twenty-four hours to repair the ruptured aneurysm and reduce the risk of rebleeding. But like two-thirds of patients with that condition, Arianna had suffered a recurrence from which she could not recover.

He recalled those dizzying days right after the funeral, the blur of time spent with his cousin in New York, and then the move back home. There could never be any other home for him, even without her. He took a bite of the second piece of toast and washed it down with coffee. And even in his melancholy state, he sensed a swell of gratitude for the village's beauty and down-home honesty and for friends who had helped him heal. Thank God for Stony Point. He would do everything in his power to keep it safe and to see that it prospered.

He was down to the last half piece of toast when he looked up to see Annie standing next to his booth. "Well, hello. How long have you been standing there?"

"Just a few seconds, but I must say, Mr. Mayor, you were deep in thought. I might have swiped the last of your breakfast and you'd never have known."

She was wearing trim white slacks and an attractive blousy top of some light rose color that made him think of beach roses along the harbor road. Her hair waved gently back like blond ripples touched with foam. Green eyes seemed to spark with greater intensity than he'd noticed before. Could be the famous Mr. Jones had something to do with that.

Well, she deserved a shot at happiness after what she'd been through. He got up and extended his arm to indicate the seat across from him. "No need to swipe. I'll buy you a cup of coffee. Care to join me?"

She slid in, leaving in her wake a faint fragrance of wild rose. Yes, she fit in nicely in Stony Point. She made it even more attractive, though unlike some women, she seemed unaware of her own merit.

"I'd love it. I'm heading for Portland this morning. Alice and I are going to make a day of it. You know, shopping, lunch. We're combining it with a visit to the library."

"A curiosity to check out?" he asked. He surprised himself by teasing her. He hadn't felt like lighthearted repartee today, but she had a way of lifting the spirit.

"Actually, Ian, I know who the boy in the photo album is. I was looking through some old issues of *The Point* and discovered that he was the son of a gardener who worked along the coast in the summer in the late eighties. In Stony Point too. His name is Cagney Torrez. He's dead, Ian."

He studied her face, which filled with sadness as she spoke the name. Surprised, he searched his mind for the name, the incident, but couldn't place it. He'd been busy falling in love with Arianna in the untroubled eighties and expanding the town's sawmill. Annie placed a newspaper clipping on the booth in front of him and smoothed it with her hand. He reached into the pocket of his shirt for his glasses.

August 12, 1989: The body of a young man was found drifting in Casco Bay 30 miles from the city of Portland. His father, an itinerant gardener who had worked in Portland and the villages of Hanover and Stony Point, identified him as sixteen-year-old Cagney Torrez. Cause of death is unknown though believed to be blunt force trauma. Stony Point officials could not comment on information that the boy might be tied to a ring of hotel thieves operating out of Portland.

"That's awful," Ian said, tracing an index finger over the tiny accompanying photo and comparing it with the snapshot Annie had just pulled from her purse. "Sure looks like the same boy, but I don't remember him. Actually, a lot of kids show up here in the summertime. We have to keep a pretty close eye on them these days, what with gang activity so prevalent." He frowned, peered again at the photo. "We're hearing more and more about that recently, and it's too close to home."

"I just can't seem to set it aside, Ian, even though it happened such a long time ago. He's dead and gone, and yet, I want to know how it happened. Such a small, lonely boy, so somber, so lonely."

That was the Annie he was getting to know. She had a great heart for people as her concern over Peggy and Wally confirmed. "I wish I could help. I can see it really troubles you. I'll be interested to know what you find out at the library, Annie." He passed the items back across the table. "Now, on other subjects, Mary Beth says you ladies are making progress on the needlework event you're planning. She's so enthralled with it all, I'm thinking of taking up crocheting myself!"

"Don't joke. Crocheting isn't just a feminine pastime. Did you know that Cornell University's math program includes a crocheted model of a pseudosphere? That's the geometric opposite of the sphere. They use it to teach hyperbolic geometry. I was reading about it online."

He stared at her, intrigued and totally baffled.

"This Latvian mathematician named Daina Taimina came up with the idea. She started crocheting these models in 1997, and now they're used to help students understand how space expands exponentially. Hyperbolic geometry!"

"That's amazing." He grinned at her. "So are you making any models of pseudospheres for the needlework fair?"

"No," she said, laughing. "That would take forever. But I am making sweaters in a stitch almost as intricate as geometry. And I promised Mary Beth I'd donate a Betsy Original if I can find one I can part with. But have you heard we've found someone with real credentials to judge the contest and to run the auction?" The rosy spots on her cheeks heightened.

"Mary Beth was mentioning something just this morning. An expert in antique jewelry all the way from New York! I am impressed."

"Yes, I was surprised he was willing to give his time like that. He. . ." She stopped, gave her head a little shake. Were those little red spots deepening?

"Well, I'm not surprised. I'm sure he finds your company enjoyable and would be eager to help you out."

"Oh, it's not like that!"

But she was too quick to protest, in his estimation. He spread his hands in a gesture of conciliation. She was an attractive woman, still vibrant, and she deserved a little romance in her life. But he just hoped she wasn't moving too fast; he knew only too well that the lonely were vulnerable.

He suppressed a frown, wondering what she knew about Jones really. "Be careful, Annie." He didn't wait for her to respond, but stood up and grabbed the check. "Great to see you. I'm off now to tend to matters of state!" He smiled and touched her lightly on her shoulder. "Take care of yourself."

~ 12 ~

When Annie returned home after a morning trip to the Portland Library, she found Dorian Jones on the porch at Grey Gables busily sanding her antique table. They had agreed he'd come and go as he had time to restore the table. Still, it gave Annie pause to find him there as though he belonged. The man of the house with a honey-do list.

"Dorian!" she exclaimed. "Hello."

He looked up from his semisquatting position beside the upturned table and smiled. "You're back," he said nonchalantly. "If you'd stayed away a little longer, I might have finished this beauty." He returned his gaze to the table admiringly.

Annie felt oddly slighted that a table received such a look of adoration. She laughed to silence this odd thought and gave an off-hand wave. "I'll just go in and freshen up. I'll make us some iced tea."

"Great," he said with a smile that did nothing to calm her nerves. He was wearing slim jeans and a white polo shirt that clung closely to his broad chest. "I'll just keep working away here." And he bent his reddish-gold head over the lucky table.

Annie and Alice had spent the morning at the Peabody Research Library. They'd left Stony Point early and covered the sixty or so miles to Portland by nine-thirty when the library opened. That way they could do their sleuthing and still have time for lunch before heading back. Alice had a Princessa Jewelry party scheduled and needed to be home at least by four.

Their mission to find out more about Cagney Torrez had not revealed anything they didn't already know. They'd found the same short report Annie had clipped from *The Point*. After wading through a gazillion reports of domestic batteries, burglaries, convenience store robberies, and bank hold-ups, they had found nothing related to the mystery teenager. Or had they?

She'd been intrigued by a report of a series of hotel thefts in which an estimated half-million dollars in cash and jewels had been taken. The perpetrators, one of whom was described as a youth, escaped by boat and mysteriously disappeared just south of Stony Point. Was it possible that Cagney Torrez was involved? Towns and villages along the coast became part of an investigation that yielded no clues, and the missing money and jewels had never been recovered.

She changed into jeans and a jersey knit shirt, ran a brush through her hair, and fled to the kitchen. She wouldn't linger at the mirror, wouldn't acknowledge that flush of anticipation and pleasure she knew would be there.

She brought the tray of iced tea and butterscotch bars out to the porch table and sat down on one of Grey Gables' white wicker chairs. A few yards away, Dorian sanded Gram's table, which on an earlier visit he had stripped down to the bare turned oak.

She could see the muscles in his arm flex with each forward stroke of the sandpaper. He wrapped his slender fingers around the table's delicate legs as he worked, almost as though he were caressing them. She felt her breath catch in her throat at the sight. What was it about a man working with his hands that was so. . .almost beautiful?

She pulled out her crocheting to distract herself while Dorian worked. The sweater was taking shape, though the intricate pattern required a great deal of concentration. Her first project had been a knitted bulky sweater for Wayne in the simplest of stitches; he claimed it was his favorite even though she'd made several mistakes.

"Be careful, Annie." Ian's words flashed into her mind. Did he mean that she shouldn't jump into a romantic relationship with someone while still grieving? That she was particularly vulnerable? That she should be very sure who she was opening herself up to? Yes, caution was a good thing. But sometimes good things got away while you were busy being too careful.

"I'm really grateful that you're taking your vacation time to do this, Dorian," she said. "And I want to thank you, too, for agreeing to help us out with our needlework fair. Mary Beth is so excited that you're going to judge our competition."

"It's a small thing to repay this community for all it offers its guests. . .serenity, beauty. . ." Dorian trailed off, continued to smooth the sandpaper over the table. "This is a rare 1660 English drop leaf," he murmured admiringly.

She looked up from her needlework. "Are you at a stopping place? I've made tea," she said hesitantly.

He straightened and set the sandpaper aside. Gently, he righted the table, which had been turned on its side while he smoothed the sculpted legs. He brushed a bit of dust off his jeans and joined her, his Pierre Cardin shirt looking fresh and new as though he'd just put it on. Shouldn't a man get sweaty when he worked?

Annie held out the plate of cookies. "How is it you know so much about tables? I thought you were into gems."

He rubbed his hands on a white handkerchief and took a butterscotch square from the plate. He fastened those curious eyes on her, eyes that even in the cloudy atmosphere glowed with golden light. "I'm a connoisseur of beautiful things," he said with a small smile.

She looked away, unnerved yet magnetized by his gaze and the possible double meaning. Each time he came, the atmosphere grew more charged. Not that he'd made any real passes or done anything to offend her. He'd been the soul of politeness, if not sometimes even seeming totally dispassionate. Was this emotional tension hers alone? Was she foolishly imagining an interest that Dorian did not feel toward her?

The air was still, the muggy afternoon heavy with impending storm, like many summer afternoons at Stony Point. Actually, it had been threatening rain all day; she and Alice had taken umbrellas to Portland just in case. But heavy cloud cover could linger like this for hours. She swung her legs up to rest them on an adjacent chair, hoping to prod her mind into a similarly relaxed position. She sighed and looked out at the ocean in the distance. It stretched unruffled, brooding beneath a lead-gray sky.

"Good thing it's under cover," she said nodding to the work in process. "It could rain soon." She sipped her tea slowly, willing herself to relax. There was nothing comfortable about Dorian Jones or the way she felt when he was around. She found that troubling, especially since she suspected it was caused by her own sense of vulnerability, the awareness that she had missed the touch of a man.

There had been no one but Wayne for as long as she could remember. It had been enough for her for all the years of their marriage and beyond. She had been content with her memories, her family, her friends. She wanted that contentment, not this unsettling yearning.

"How was your visit to the big city?" he asked, propping one leg over the other.

His head inclined toward her, and she saw that his blond hair was darker toward the roots. Likely it had been bleached by the sun. Her own grew lighter in summertime too. "It was good," she said. "Alice and I went to the Chez Henri for lunch."

"Great spot," he affirmed. Of course he would know it. He wasn't the burger-on-the-go kind of guy. Anyone who could afford Gucci loafers and Pierre Cardin shirts would know Portland's upscale restaurants. He'd mentioned appointments in the area; no doubt these took him there as well as to such places as Augusta and Camden.

"Our waiter had cherry red hair that stood up in peaks on his head. Skinny as a rail and dressed in black, he looked like a rocket ready to blast off, or like one that just did!"

"Sounds explosive," he rejoined. "Well, you can see anything in the city these days. In New York it's hard to tell if people are dressing for the office or a Halloween party."

"I guess in your line of work, you see everything. What's

it like, those big auctions where some obscure item in a closet sells for thousands of dollars?"

He laughed a little; he seldom laughed, and when he did, as now, it didn't quite reach his eyes. She felt a rush of compassion quite apart from any romantic leaning. This was a man unaccustomed to peace or real joy. Not unlike many in the world, she supposed.

"Oh, it's just like a big flea market, only the stakes are higher. I make it a practice to stay away when the crowds come with their dubious treasures. You can see anything there: toys, paintings, armoires, chamber pots, Barbie dolls, carousel horses. Good ones can go for seventy thousand dollars and up."

"It looks so exciting on television," she said.

"They only show you the highlights, not the long hours standing in line, the tedium. The majority of stuff turns out to be worthless." He paused. "I've gone through piles of jewelry that was nothing but paste, stuff your waiter might wear to a costume party. But once in a while you land a real find." He took a long swallow of tea and put the glass down with finality, as though he no longer wished to talk about the subject.

"Where did you learn about such things?" Early on he'd mentioned a university in the West. "You said you went to. . . where was it?"

"Phoenix," he supplied. "But that was years ago. Mostly I learned from experience, and from people like your grandmother who understood beautiful things and took care of them."

Annie regarded him curiously. "I don't think she had

any idea of what things were worth," she said thoughtfully. "She always loved a gracious line, the impress of fine wood, but she wasn't interested in how much things cost." A picture of Gram placing her Aster Blue china in the cupboard flashed into her mind. She could see the hands, grown a bit knobby from arthritis but still beautiful, still sure, tucking a paper liner under each china plate to avoid scratching.

" 'A thing of beauty is a joy forever,' " she would quote and then add, "so long as you take care of it." Annie could remember sitting on a dining room chair looking up at Gram, watching her hands move in their graceful dance. She remembered Gram saying, "Relationships are like that too. The good ones are worth keeping, and they must be treated with tender care."

The memory sliced through her with a sudden mix of pain and joy, and she couldn't speak. She looked across at Dorian. What had he been saying that had sparked this memory? She wanted to stop the pain of missing Gram, the sadness of knowing those dear hands would never touch hers again.

A low rumble broke the spell, and a sudden gust of wind swooped up the napkins she had placed on the table. A streak of lightning and then rain began with startling swiftness—not a drop or two, but a quick needle-like assault. She scrambled up. "It's coming in at a slant! We'll be drenched. Come on!" She glanced around looking for Boots, who until this moment she had not realized was gone. She hoped she'd find a safe, dry place.

Dorian ran to throw the tarp over the gateleg table as the wind blew up with the intensity of a nor'easter. Annie could barely hold the screen door steady until he made it inside. Then together they pushed the outer door shut as a deafening clap of thunder crashed.

Breathless with exertion and the suddenness of the storm, Annie realized that Dorian was right next to her, leaning on the door. The fragrance of his cologne enveloped her, its wild, primitive aroma heightened by wind and moisture.

"We made it. Are you all right?" Dorian asked.

His hands clasped her shoulders; his face was so close to hers she could feel his breath. Piercing eyes beneath dark furrowed brows peered into hers. His hands seemed to burn through her knit shirt, and she could feel her pulse racing with something very like fear. Passion? No.

Shaken, she pulled away, laughing to cover the intensity of the moment. "You never think a storm can come up that quickly until you experience it. I better check the windows. Boots!" she called. "You here, Boots?" She scanned the living room, the dining room, the kitchen, across the hall to the family room, watching for a trace of gray tail or white paws. Dorian followed, helping her close windows as they went. "She doesn't like storms. I hope she's scuttled under a bed or something." It was becoming clear that, whether from jealousy or some feline distrust of men, Boots did not like Dorian.

"He'll be fine. Cats can take care of themselves," he said, somewhat callously.

"She," Annie corrected. She decided to forgive his apparent lack of concern for Boots. She frowned. "Usually when a storm flares up this suddenly, it dies away quickly and the sun comes out all innocent and sweet. It won't last long."

"I hope you're right. I have an appointment in a little while." He paused, glanced at her, and then seemed to study something she couldn't see. "But it's my good luck to be stranded in this beautiful old house," he said, standing still and looking around wonderingly. His restive eyes took in every detail from floor to ceiling. "There's that fabulous rococo table."

She was astounded. He remembered it. Had he and Gram sat in this very room, talked together over tea? "Do you want to see the rest of the house? Come on, we'll close the upstairs windows and I'll show you around."

"Lead on," he said eagerly, as yet another burst of thunder roared.

He certainly had an eye for detail, but that must be what made him good as an appraiser of antiques. She could no doubt learn a lot from him, though she felt nervous having a man inside her house. She laughed at her hesitation. What century was she living in anyway? "Same woodwork I remember from when I was a child," she said as casually as she could. "Gram wasn't much for changes."

He said nothing at that, but he had a look of near reverence on his face as he stood at the door while she closed a bedroom window. He was facing the attic door. "I love old houses with attics. Mind if I look?"

She'd gotten rid of some of the attic clutter and wasn't quite as ashamed of its appearance. "Not at all," she murmured and led the way up. "I used to love to sit up here in a storm when I spent summers with Gram."

His eyes traveled from the shabby old sofa with its rainbow afghan to the ceiling. He nodded appreciatively. "Crown molding." He pointed to the uppermost cornice at the attic's peak. "That is magnificent apex flashing. They don't make that scalloped edging anymore. I assume this is the original woodwork." He paused to glance her way and then returned his gaze to the cornice. "Late-eighteenth-century walnut, isn't it?"

She supposed a connoisseur of Victorian homes could be fascinated by such features. Frankly, she had no idea; woodwork wasn't high on her interest list. "I've been going through boxes and drawers," Annie said, moving into the center of the attic. "Sorry for the mess. You never know what people save, and Gram was a saver." Dorian followed. He gazed around at the chaos and then upward once more to the cornice he found so interesting.

Dorian's presence gave the room a strange, heightened ambience. It wasn't a comfortable feeling, but at the same time it was exciting. Puzzled, she cast about for a suitable comment. "I was looking for one of Gram's original needle-work pieces," she stammered. "I promised Mary Beth I'd donate one for the auction. Oh, that's the one I thought I might part with. Right there." She motioned to a 16×20 canvas propped up on one end of the couch. "It's rather dark and foreboding, not my favorite of her many needlework paintings. That's how I think of them, you know, because they're truly works of art. . ." She stopped, aware that she'd been rambling on nervously.

The tapestry showed Stony Point's distinctive coastline and Butler's Lighthouse jutting out from its peak. It was one of Gram's early works, done while the old keeper's quarters was still attached. It had long since been torn down and the lighthouse remodeled. Gram had used heavy gray and lavender threads that provoked a somber, almost frightening quality. Annie didn't particularly like it; it didn't show the beauty of the old lighthouse or inspire any warmth. She studied it, aware that she was frowning. Yes, she'd be willing to part with that one.

Suddenly she realized that Dorian was staring oddly at the canvas. He looked pale in the attic's dim light, and his eyes had gone dull and flat. He had drawn his hands out of his pockets; they were suspended in midair.

"Oh, do you like it?" she asked.

He took a step back, cleared his throat. "It's. . .quite. . . uh, unusual," he said with a somewhat patronizing air.

"Do you think anyone will want it?" she asked.

He stuffed his hands back in his pockets and said nonchalantly, "Well, you never know. People buy the strangest things." He took another step back toward the hallway. He seemed disconcerted, and those sharp eyes no longer sought the upper molding. "Like I said, this is a great old house, and I had a small part in helping maintain it all those years ago." He broke off. "Well, it was a long time ago."

She followed him back down the stairs, aware that he seemed eager to go. True to the nature of sudden violent storms, this one had dissipated and the rain had stopped. They stood at the front door, looking out at the rain-washed view.

"Yes," Dorian said reflectively, "I felt quite at home doing odd jobs around the house with your grandmother humming as she worked in the kitchen." He put his hand on the screen door's latch, gave it a little twist, and then let it go.

He turned to face her, bending his handsome head toward her. "I'll stain the table tomorrow; I've heard the weather's going to be good." Then he gently cupped his hands around her shoulders and looked deeply into her eyes. The brush of his lips on her cheek was so sudden that all logical thought vanished. Then quickly he was gone. She watched him sprint across the wet grass and down the path.

It was several minutes before she returned to the thought she'd had just before that breathless moment, before his quick parting kiss. Gram humming? She'd never heard Gram hum in the kitchen or anyplace else. Not even in church. She couldn't carry a tune in a bushel basket and she knew it. "I have a voice like a crow," she used to say. "And I never use it in polite company."

~ 13 ~

"Hello, old fella," Ian said, breaking his usual rule and accepting Tartan's furry front paws in greeting. The dog lapped Ian's face with his little red tongue and danced in happy expectation. Ian had gone home to give Tartan a walk in the middle of the day. There were advantages to living close to the office, though at times his schedule had meant Tartan had to wait, which he usually did with admirable self-control. Now he was tugging at his leash that hung on the wall next to the door.

"Hang on! We're going; I promise." He thumbed through the mail that had been delivered that day. Bills, ads, and assorted other junk mail. Not even a letter from his cousin in upstate New York. He dropped it on the hall table on top of the rest of the week's unappealing offerings and was aware of the silence of the house. Even Tartan's excited panting couldn't fill the emptiness.

Not so long ago, Arianna would have met him at the door. Instead of furry paws, tender arms would encircle his neck. Warm lips would cover his in a quick but decisive kiss. Sometimes they'd walk their pets together, she with Yolanda, her demure little Yorkie, and he with Tartan straining on the leash. Sometimes they'd take long strolls along the ocean, watch the tides come and go, talk about the new play she was working on or about the business of Stony Point.

"Cut it out," he said, snapping the leash on the squirming animal. But he wasn't speaking so much to his well-bred Schnauzer as to himself. Was it to be like this every time her birthday rolled around? Or every time he saw a German chocolate cake in the bakery window? Or in a thousand little unguarded moments of the day or night?

He had no right to feel sorry for himself, he argued inwardly. His life was good; he had a host of friends and a community that looked to him for peace and prosperity. Mostly, he'd been able to meet their expectations because he'd been surrounded by hard-working, upstanding neighbors who stayed true to long-established traditions of honesty and integrity. He could depend on them; it was an honor to be involved in governing under such conditions.

Arianna had come to love Stony Point as much as he did. A big-city girl, Arianna had quickly adopted Maine's warm-hearted citizens. And she had brought the excitement of the theater, fostered art and music among their friends and neighbors. Ian had been touched by the flood of cards and flowers and casseroles that followed his return after a brief hiatus in New York. He had come home. Perhaps their tenacious good will, their sturdy friendship had drawn him. More than calling him home, it had in large part healed him.

One never completely recovered from such a loss, he supposed. You just thanked God for the moments of exhilaration and contentment that have been yours and prayed for strength to endure the lonely times. He'd seen that spirit in others such as Annie Dawson, and he marveled at her warmth and kindness. That was the key. Looking morosely inward was destructive, but reaching out to others had the power to heal even the deepest sorrow.

Reverend Wallace liked to quote Victor Hugo, the great nineteenth-century French writer. One quote in particular always inspired him: "Have courage for the great sorrows of life and patience for the small ones; when you have laboriously accomplished your daily tasks, go to sleep in peace. God is awake."

But the day wasn't over, and he had a mission that had been fomenting in his mind ever since he'd talked to Mary Beth and later that day to Annie. It involved one Dorian Jones, purported expert in antiques.

"He's a trained gemologist," Mary Beth had said, her intelligent eyes bright with excitement. "And he has connections with some of the best auction houses in the country, even Christie's and Sotheby's." She had reverently whispered the two famous names.

Annie certainly seemed high on him. Her face had lit up when she mentioned how Mr. Jones had been helping out at Grey Gables. So why was an esteemed antiques dealer bothering to fill in for Wally Carson as handyman's helper? On the surface, he supposed, it was easy enough to understand. Annie was a lovely, available woman. Mr. Jones, traveling alone, was likely similarly unattached. And he might just want to help out of loyalty to Annie's grandmother, Ian admitted to himself somewhat grudgingly.

Ian recalled his brief look at Jones when he'd gone by Annie's with a request for help on a local campaign. He'd been surprised to see the man up on a ladder, pounding loose a window shutter that apparently needed refitting.

He was undeniably handsome, with dark blond hair of an odd reddish-gold hue and muscles that showed he worked out regularly. Didn't quite fit with an antique dealer's persona, he'd thought at the time, but he'd shrugged that off. Ian was admittedly suspicious of strangers, though he tried not to be.

He'd been put off but recognized his innate penchant to protect Stony Point's citizens, even the new ones who'd taken up permanent residence. And Annie was definitely worth protecting. She'd quickly gained the affection of just about everyone. And his own, he had to admit. So why was he balking at this opportunity for Annie to find companionship—maybe even a little romance? She'd been alone long enough and deserved the attention of a successful suitor. If that's what he was.

"We're going to make one stop before we head home, boy," Ian said, looping Tartan's leash through a bar in a bicycle stand. The Maplehurst Inn had one of several bike stands in town, placed there mainly for the summer visitors who often rented bikes to get around the village. "Be a good boy," he cautioned and ruffled the dog's short, stiff hair.

Maplehurst was a well-established inn with only two levels and some two dozen tastefully fitted rooms. Recently remodeled, it boasted a new stone façade that complemented its buff-colored vinyl siding. Dark green canvas awnings gave it an old-world touch. The owners who'd taken it over two years ago had also turned the coffee-and-sandwich café into a full-fledged dining room. White tablecloths, real flowers. Candles and crystal for the evening hour, no doubt, though Ian hadn't yet dined at Maplehurst.

Ian paused at the gleaming glass entryway, feeling awkward. He could hardly charge in, ask the room number, and knock on Mr. Jones' door—even if the proprietor were disposed to give that information. At three o'clock in the afternoon, the antique dealer was not likely to be in anyway. Ian frowned. And once he did confront him, what was he going to say?

At least he could have a cup of coffee and think about it. Inside the dining room, lights were dim, and only a few patrons sat at the round mahogany tables set with sparkling glasses and silver wrapped in linen. The place was posh and clean, but it was a far cry from the Cup and Saucer's warmth and liveliness.

At the rear of the dining room, a solitary figure sat engrossed in a newspaper. He was tall, with copper-colored hair, and wore a suit coat of some dark fabric, which even at a distance Ian could see was finely tailored. Stony Point regulars never wore suit coats in the afternoon. The man appeared relaxed, broad shoulders slightly convex, one leg crossed over the other at the ankle. Ian needed no second guess. This had to be Mr. Dorian Jones.

He looked up when Ian entered, his dark brows rising slightly. Ian nodded to a waiter who suddenly appeared, took a menu, and approached the man at the rear. He put out a hand. "I'm Ian Butler. Don't think I've had the pleasure."

The man straightened but did not rise. A surprised smile started but was over before it could spread. He extended his hand. Then, as though suddenly remembering his manners, he rose, cleared his throat. "Dorian Jones. You would be Ian Butler, the mayor of this excellent town. The pleasure is mine." His diction was perfect, his gaze steady, though cool and appraising. Pausing only briefly, he indicated a chair at his table. "Care to join me?"

Ian sat, pulled in his chair, and looked up at the waiter. "Just coffee for me. Thanks." He took his time unrolling the silverware and clearing the spot in front of him, glad for small gestures that gave him time to collect his thoughts. Something about Dorian Jones was unnerving. It might be that he had a height advantage of some three inches or that his appearance was too perfect.

"How are you enjoying Stony Point?" Ian began, folding his hands on the table and looking his companion in the eye.

"It's even better than I remember it, Mr. Mayor. It's a real up-and-coming town. Real progress has taken place. No doubt that's to the credit of insightful leadership."

Ian felt his jaw tighten. Flattery always made him uncomfortable, though he was used to hearing it. "You've been here before?" Mary Beth had told him about Betsy Holden's young helper two decades earlier, but it was as good an opener as he could think of. Besides, he wanted to hear Dorian's take.

"I was just a kid then. Needed work to earn money for college. Mrs. Holden was good enough to let me help out at Grey Gables. A fine old house. She had quite an eye for fine antiques."

"Yes," Ian said thoughtfully and hesitated. He was sure his companion had more to say.

"I think that's where my interest in antiques began. You know, of course, that I'm an antique dealer of sorts. Gems mostly. I've agreed to help out at the event Ms. Brock is sponsoring. It's the least I could do, considering what this town has given me."

Ian pursed his lips, wondering exactly what that was. After a moment he said, "Yes, you've made quite a hit with the Hook and Needle Club. This is to be their first such event; they're quite eager that it succeed. They probably hope it will become an annual event, like the Fourth of July celebration."

Ian's coffee arrived, offering a pause in their careful conversation. Dorian resumed his relaxed position, recrossing his leg. The motion showed off Argyle socks and a thick mass of very dark hair between the top of the sock and his pant leg. It was a poor match for the distinctly reddish-gold hair on his head. Ian glanced at an arm resting on the table but saw no hint of hair around his gold Rolex.

"I understand Mrs. Holden was quite an artist with her cross-stitch canvases. It's a shame I've never seen one at Christie's or Sotheby's." Dorian rearranged himself in his chair, assumed a more businesslike posture.

"How long have you been with them?" Ian asked casually. "The auction houses, I mean."

Dorian shrugged rather grandly, lowered his pale eyes of no color that Ian could discern. "A number of years. Actually I work free-lance for quite a few houses. My interests are quite broad." He cleared his throat, swallowed the last bit of coffee in his cup, and pushed his chair back.

An evasive answer if Ian ever heard one. And nothing he'd heard or seen had lessened his sense of caution about Mr. Dorian Jones. He'd have to look more closely into his background. Jones was obviously eager to put an end to their discussion, but Ian wasn't ready to release him just yet. "You. . .uh. . .planning to be in Maine long?"

"I've just come for the summer. A bit of a vacation. There's nothing like the ocean and a rocky coastline. . .and of course the friendly citizens of this rather remarkable town." He started to rise. "I hope you'll forgive me. I have some calls to make." He extended a hand that felt cool and slightly damp. "And allow me to compliment you on the improvements that have been made over the years."

Ian rose too, trying to squelch his distaste over the all-too-obvious flattery. "You've been making some improvements yourself, I understand," he said with a nonchalance he didn't feel. "Annie tells me you're sort of pinch-hitting for Wally Carson. Since he's broken his arm and all."

Dorian raised one heavy eyebrow but quickly smiled to cover any surprise he might have felt. "Like I said, I feel I owe her grandmother for her kindness to me when I was just a kid. She gave me a job, helped me get started in my field. Annie needed my help; I'm glad to give her a hand."

Ian nodded. "We're all proud of our Annie," he said, looking directly into Dorian's disturbing eyes. "She's become quite an important part of our community." He wanted to say that if the man's intentions were anything but honorable, he'd have the whole town on his case—and that Ian himself would be the first to break his neck. Instead he finished, "I'm sure she'll be glad for help. Grey Gables is a big place to handle."

Dorian said nothing but picked up the check at both places. "Allow me," he said succinctly. "Nice talking to you, Mr. Butler."

Ian watched him walk out, then followed him at several paces. The man had said all the right words, carried himself like a gentleman, but Ian didn't trust him any farther than he could throw him. The frustrating thing was that he had no rational basis for his distaste.

Nevertheless, Tartan would be delighted to know there would be one more stop before the walk ended. Chief Edwards hadn't been around long, but police files were carefully kept. Ian narrowed his hazel eyes and jiggled the keys in his pockets. It wouldn't hurt to dig back a few years and see what turned up.

~ 14 ~

"Daddy, tell Madeline a story. Please!"

Emily screwed up her short nose until her blue eyes nearly disappeared in her round little face. Tinges of gold highlighted her curls, especially the damp ones around her head. Shell-like ears peeked through her hair. Her eyes, a mix of Peggy's cornflower blue and Wally's dark brown ones, reminded him of the cobalt ocean beneath a summer sky.

"Madeline says she can't go to sleep until she hears a story, Daddy!"

Emily wiggled Madeline under his nose, pretending a wild dance, which was not quite ballerina style but more like a struggling Atlantic cod on the end of a teaser. He gently pressed the cloth doll back toward her. "Okay, okay. Just let me think a minute. Once upon a time. . ." he began slowly, deliberately.

Wally knew she loved his stories, which he made up as he went rather than struggle through a book. He left that for Peggy, who tonight was resting on the couch with a headache. She'd been on her feet all day at the Cup and Saucer and had asked Wally to put Emily to bed. He never minded bedtime with Emily, but tonight he was so fidgety he wasn't sure he could even think straight. He'd retell her favorite story.

He glanced at his dark windbreaker that lay over the

back of Emily's pink-cushioned chair in readiness for his ten o'clock meeting. The package he'd agreed to deliver was no bigger than a box of replacement checks from the bank, but it had been burning in his pocket since noon when the Louis II had pulled into harbor.

"Daddy, Madeline's waiting for her story!"

"Once upon a time," he began again, "there was a beautiful dancer named Madeline. She had long silken hair piled on top of her head—just right for wearing a ring of beautiful flowers in. She had long, dancing legs that never got tired. One day, just before it was time to go up onstage..." He gave a long, dramatic pause. "...she lost one of her slippers."

Emily's eyes grew large. With small, delicate fingers, she stroked the doll's pink-ribbon shoes. Then she exclaimed, "Oh, no! Not her slippers! Madeline can't dance without her magic shoes, Daddy."

"I know," Wally said. "So poor Madeline looked everywhere. She looked in her dressing room with the big star on it, and under her chair. She looked in her little suitcase. She ran outside and looked on the sidewalk and under the trees. She looked everywhere she could think of, but she could not find her dancing slipper. Madeline began to cry. Her tears fell on her shiny costume and onto her poor bare foot."

"Then what, Daddy?" Emily pulled the doll tightly to her chest as though to comfort it, rocking back and forth.

"The audience shouted, 'Where is Madeline? We want to see Madeline dance, or else we want our money back!' They began to holler, 'We want Madeline! We want Madeline!'

And poor Madeline cried and cried. Then suddenly, her very best friend in the whole world came running into her dressing room, and in her hand she held. . .guess what?"

"Her pink slipper!" Emily shouted triumphantly.

"Yes," said Wally, "And do you know who her very best friend in the whole world is who found her slipper?"

"Who, Daddy? Who?"

"Emily, that's who!" And he grabbed his little girl up in a huge bear hug. It was part of the game; he'd told the story before, and this was the best part, the part she always waited for that ended in a chaos of giggles. Then he would tuck her in with Madeline beside her and draw the covers over both of them.

He switched off the lamp, picked up his jacket carefully, and left the room. He smiled in spite of his nervousness, knowing his little girl was tucked safely in her bed. The soapy smell of her, fresh from her bedtime bath, clung to his neck where her small arms had curled around him.

He tiptoed past Peggy, who at nine o'clock lay curled up on the couch. In one hand she clutched a quilt block of a red-haired mermaid partially embroidered. The other hand hung over the edge inert. She was asleep, but Wally knew one sound from Emily would send her bolt upright.

He hoped she wouldn't wake when he returned later. He always went out for a walk before bed, but tonight it would take longer. He had to get to the lighthouse, and because of his disabled car he'd have to walk. Make that *run*. He didn't want to hold onto the package one more minute than he had to.

He'd been on edge ever since he'd agreed to accept the

delivery for Dorian Jones. He wasn't sure why. The request was reasonable, Wally supposed. Jones didn't know exactly when the Louis II would arrive, so rather than hang around the harbor all day, he'd asked Wally to pick it up. Wally spent the day on the dock anyway. Besides, Jones had an appointment and wouldn't get back until tonight. The rich antique dealer from New York was counting on him.

Earlier that day, at a time when a bevy of boats crowded in to unload their traps, the twenty-foot Louis II had cruised into the harbor. It was a typical lobster boat with a round bottom and a double-wedge hull. In the open-decked cockpit aft, a man waited, while another stepped off with a line of traps.

"Wally Carson." It was a statement more than a question. In bibs and boots, a man approached. He was fifty or so, a grizzly, bearded hulk with a messy mustache. He looked like a lot of guys. Wally had never seen anyone from the Louis II before, but this man knew who he was. It had struck him as odd to be recognized so quickly, but then Jones had said the guy with the package would find him.

"That's me."

"Grizzly" separated one of the traps from his line, handed it to Wally and turned back to his boat, heavy boots sloshing on the wet pier.

Wally had taken the trap inside the fish house and removed the small package, which was wrapped in brown paper and tied with a thin, strong cord. He'd tucked it into an inner jacket pocket that he kept in the gear closet and gone back to work. He hadn't looked at the package again. But he'd thought about it.

What kind of antique came in a box small enough to fit inside his coat? A feather-light box at that. Jewelry, maybe? The guy did something with gems, appraised them for big companies. Something like that. Still, Wally didn't like being responsible for a package valuable enough to be camouflaged in a lobster trap and handed over in secret. What if. . .? But no, Dorian Jones was a nice guy—educated, well bred. He'd been really polite. Besides, he was Annie's friend; he wouldn't be involved with anything shady or underhanded.

Now as Wally walked briskly past the quiet strip of sandy beach, he silently talked to himself. *So what's the big deal? It's a package. You deliver it; you keep the quick two hundred dollars and that's it. None of your business what's inside.*

So what was making him so antsy he'd not even been able to concentrate when Peggy and Emily talked to him over their dinner of stew and biscuits?

"Long day?" Peg had asked, tipping her head to one side and puckering her lips slightly in a gesture of pity. "You look puny." That was her word for not feeling good or for being tired. She'd asked him to put Emily to bed because she'd felt puny and just wanted to crash on the couch.

"Nah. Not so bad, but there was a lot of cleaning and hauling today. Good day for fishing. What about you? Lotta tourists crowding in?"

"Heavens, yes! I think the whole world's decided to vacation in Stony Point!" She flopped back on the chair and splayed her fingers out in a gesture of exhaustion. "Can I get more coffee, Miss? What about my apple dumpling, Miss? Can I have the Friday special with a baked potato instead of fries?" She mimicked the day's customers, her pretty face animated.

It was no wonder Peggy was the most popular waitress at the Cup and Saucer. She had a way of making everyone feel he or she was the most important person in the café. Her quick wit and charming ways endeared her to everyone. He still had to pinch himself every now and then to believe she really was married to him. How he wished he could buy her the things she deserved.

Wouldn't she be tickled when he brought home his paycheck from Todd and added the extra two hundred! He could explain it easily enough. He'd put in some overtime; besides, Todd Butler was generous like Ian. Still, he didn't like keeping things from Peggy. And then there was Emily, his sweet little girl they'd waited so long for.

"Daddy, I got the biggest smiley face ever from my teacher today. She said my ballet dancer was the prettiest one she'd ever seen. I drew her just like Madeline." Her blue eyes shone over the rim of her glass.

Wally's heart swelled with pride and love. Emily could talk of nothing but dancing these days. She was patient for a six-year-old. She didn't beg and plead and scream for what she wanted like some kids. But, darn it all, she shouldn't have to wait! Very soon now they would enroll her in that dance class at Myra's. He couldn't wait to see her surprised little face.

"Do you think the car will be ready tomorrow, Wally?" Peggy asked.

He shrugged. "Not sure what's wrong with it yet." He was getting pretty good at one-handed driving, especially since he had broken his left arm, not his good right one.

It was fully dark now as he walked along the coast toward the lighthouse. A weak moon slipped in and out of gray cloud cover; mild swells lapped against ragged cliffs.

As a kid, he'd hung out around the lighthouse after dark. Ruefully, he recalled those troubled teen years when he'd drifted like an unmoored skiff. He and Jem hadn't been bad kids really. Maybe a little bit wild. They'd swipe buoys after dark, exchange them with their own so they could haul in a bigger catch the next day. Or they'd party out on the tip. Sometimes they'd sneak into the old keeper's cottage, leaving one of the guys as lookout. At least until village officials began patrolling the point. Eventually they'd torn down the old eyesore and refurbished the light. That had been about the time he'd crashed up Jem's car and landed in the hospital.

He'd been glad to see that creepy shack go. There wasn't much good to remember about those long-ago days and the stuff they did when no one was looking. Peggy was back in his life, in his heart, and he was determined to make something of himself. Wally set his jaw, squared his shoulders. But the movement tightened the bulge in his jacket pocket.

Why did he have this sense that something wasn't quite right about this job? What was it about the golden-haired New Yorker that made him edgy? He looked around as he neared the grove of trees jutting out from the shoal of rocks, but he saw no sign of Dorian Jones or anyone else.

It was eerie this time of night. Strange how everything changed. A few hours earlier the dock had been bustling with activity. The harbor burgeoned with fishermen, boats and traps, and all of the equipment of the industry so important to the people who lived along the coast. Then, too, there were the tourists who wanted to watch lobstermen at work and, of course, eat the fruits of their labor.

The coastal road was deserted. He knew it was policed from time to time, but Wally hadn't even spotted the Marine Patrol. They would likely be more active after midnight. He shivered a little as the wind whipped up a swirl of sand under his feet. It was only ten o'clock but it felt like midnight. He just wanted to hand over the package and get out of there.

Suddenly a figure stepped out of the shadows and came toward him. It appeared disembodied in the dim glow of the crescent moon that outlined only a white face and a blond head. Then a glitter of eyes peered above the upturned collar of a dark coat.

Dorian Jones, dressed in dark pants and a navy peacoat, raised one white hand in a casual greeting. "Right on time," he said smiling. He clapped Wally on the shoulder. "Good man! I knew I could count on you."

Wally began to reach into his jacket for the package, but Dorian slipped an arm through his and steered him around as though they were good pals out for a stroll.

"Let's walk out to the coast road," he said with an easy smile. His teeth were very white, and his smile wide enough that Wally noticed one gold tooth on an upper-left molar. "My car's up there. I'll give you a ride back."

He dropped Wally's arm, and together they walked past the shrouded point and up the rocky path until, in the shine of moonlight, Wally could see a dark sedan at the side of the road, its lights extinguished. It was parked in the shelter of an outgrowth of trees. Wally would have preferred to walk home, but he still had the package.

"Hop in." The voice was friendly, relaxed. They might be two old friends who just happened to meet as they walked along the beach.

Dorian Jones steered the car easily onto the road, large white hands wrapped around the wheel. Wally saw that he wore rings on the third finger of each hand. The rings gleamed in the dim light of the dashboard, and Wally had the odd feeling of being somewhere outside himself, somewhere totally alien. He didn't like it. He felt almost. . .what? Afraid? But why? There was really no good reason. He squirmed in the slippery vinyl seat, felt twinges of discomfort in his broken arm. They drove in silence for half a mile and turned around a wide curve.

"So. . ." Dorian said. "Any problems?"

Wally shook his head. "Got your package right here," he said uncomfortably, reaching into his pocket.

"Just toss it in the glove compartment there," Dorian said and didn't even look over as Wally pressed the button and pulled the brown-wrapped package from his jacket pocket. The glove box was empty but for a small white envelope. "That's yours. Just a little bonus for helping me out." His tone was warm, relaxed. "Go on. Take it."

A bonus on top of the two hundred he already gave him? Wally swallowed. He took the envelope, tucked it into his pocket and shut the compartment door. The package out of his hands, he felt a wave of relief but tensed again when he realized that Dorian had turned onto his street and was driving up the short road leading directly to his house. The guy knew where he lived! He hadn't asked the number; he'd driven straight to it. Had Annie told him?

Remember, not a word to anyone. Not your friends or Annie and not even that sweet Peggy of yours. The warning Jones had given when they'd made their agreement returned to Wally now with sinister suddenness. "How'd you know. . ." he broke off, stopped by something hard in those strange, glittery eyes. Wally's hand trembled on the door handle. He just wanted to go home.

The expression on his companion's face changed again, the way a turbulent ocean could suddenly grow quiet and still, Wally thought. A slow smile spread across Jones' handsome face. "You're a good man, Wally. Annie said you could be trusted. I may need some help again and. . ."

"No," Wally said emphatically. "That is. . .I. . .I don't think I can do that." He stared straight ahead, hearing the unreasoning fear in his own voice.

A brief silence ensued and then the calm, cultured accents resumed. "I see."

Wally could think of nothing else to say that would make his refusal seem logical. The silence seemed to stretch on endlessly.

"I see," Jones crooned again thoughtfully. Nothing in his tone indicated that he was in the least upset or angered by Wally's response.

"Sorry, I can't. . ." But once again, Wally could not artic-ulate his hesitation, his misgivings about having anything further to do with Dorian Jones. He creeped him out! What did Annie see in him?

"I understand you're a busy guy. . .with a family to take care of." Jones stressed that last phrase with carefully drawn out syllables. "Well, no problem, but let's keep this between ourselves. You take care now. Take care of Emily—and that sweet Peggy."

Wally pushed out of the car without looking again at the face, which he knew had become wary, like an eerily calm sea churning angrily beneath the surface.

～ 15 ～

Fingers poised over her Mac keyboard, Amy Martinelli stared at the image of the willowy model on the screen. Stick-thin and poured into a V-neck black sheath, the pale figure stared back as though defying descriptive powers. Amy bit her lip, frowned at the long voile drape sweeping behind the figure. Like a peacock's tail, it wrapped around shapely ankles in stiletto heels. The catalog copy was due tomorrow, and she still had a dozen more blurbs to write that would stimulate sales. Her descriptions in the catalog would hopefully entice customers to buy.

Amy sighed and looked absently around the large back room of Melanie's design company. Functional and neat with a dozen cubicles, the design label above the door read simply "Melanie." But nothing was simple about the life of Melanie Martinelli or the people who worked for her. When she returned from. . .where was it this time? Cozumel? Tenerife? . . .her mother would expect every detail of her new fashion line attended to and no doubt would reward her trusted staff with fat bonuses.

Amy had no interest in fashion or bonuses. She had long ago escaped the whole dreary business, only to find herself cast back into it, at least for the moment. Helplessness engulfed her. It was no new feeling but one always just an arm's length away.

"The costume is rather indescribable, isn't it?"

Amy jumped, realizing someone was looking over her shoulder.

"It's nearly 12:30. Want to grab some lunch?"

Everett Graber, medium height, soft-spoken, book-ish, put a hand on the back of her chair. He raised one dark eyebrow and gave her a hopeful smile. Ev Graber had seemed safe enough to Amy. He had offered friendship and didn't press her with ardent advances she was unprepared to handle. They'd been dating for quite a while, gone to the symphony, movies, walks in the parks, and even the Ground Zero Museum Workshop, which had left them both too depressed for the dinner they'd planned to enjoy afterward.

Amy frowned into the screen and closed the page with a quick click of her mouse. Ev's work as one of Melanie's accountants was likely as dull as her copywriting chores, and she felt sorry for him. She liked him, too. He was thoughtful and gentle and devoted to his little boy, who shared his Second Avenue apartment. Last week Ev had broken a date because Peter had gotten sick at school and had to be sent home.

She looked at him now, sad to disappoint him. "I'm sorry, Ev. I'm so behind in my work. I've brought a sandwich. I think I'd better work through lunch today. How's Peter?"

An impish grin and dark button eyes flashed into her mind as she spoke Peter's name. The little boy had a slow, sweet smile like his father's, but no doubt his thatch of black hair and olive skin had been inherited from his mother, who had lost a battle with leukemia shortly after her baby had been born. Brazilian born, she had been a model and worked for Melanie. Beautiful, gregarious, with snapping chestnut eyes, her life had been cut short, and gentle Peter was left without a mother.

"He's fine. Back in school and driving me crazy."

"Good. I mean good that he's better; not that he's driving you crazy." Amy laughed to dispel the pain creeping from her chest to her shoulder blades. Odd aches and pains were part and parcel of depression, so the experts said. She wouldn't be good company for Ev today, in any case. "Let's do lunch tomorrow," she said, "when I get this stuff off my plate." She swept a hand toward the computer monitor now showing her screen saver, a serene sandy cove bounded by undulating blue waters. At the distant peak, a lighthouse rose from a rocky shoal where emerald green pines pierced the sky.

"Okay," he said. He took a few steps away, paused and turned around, hands in the pockets of his gray slacks. His brow furrowed beneath dark hair that was graying slightly at the temples. He fixed concerned brown eyes on hers. "Everything all right?"

The gentleness in his voice made her swallow hard. She nodded and quickly returned her gaze to the screen, blinking against sudden tears that turned the blue water and the ivory-hued lighthouse into a rippling haze.

The picture might have been a scene straight out of Stony Point. Why she continued to keep it as her screen saver she couldn't articulate. It had the power to send her into feelings of near joy or doldrums of deep sorrow. Part of her yearned to be there and to visit with Auntie Beth. (Though she'd long outgrown childhood, Mary Beth Brock was still "Auntie Beth.") Yet another part of her recoiled at the real sight of those blue, blue waters and golden sand.

Was it possible *he* was still out there somewhere? Perhaps waiting for her? There where her youth and innocence, her very heart, had been shattered? Could he have survived the fall from that rocky ledge into the swirling waters below? She hadn't come to his defense, couldn't even look as the terrible fight continued and the ocean splashed over the jagged cliffs. Why had she run away? She had been petrified by that hulking figure, that terrible man he had feared so. When Cagney had pushed her toward the woods, the terror in his eyes had been palpable, transferring itself into her heart with irrevocable power. She might have been able to help him—to save him. *Oh, Cagney, I am so sorry.*

Sometimes she would imagine that he was still alive, that he had gone on to live some kind of life somewhere, perhaps with a wife and children. She would dream that he still recalled a starry-eyed girl who had loved him, who still wore the beautiful ruby necklace he'd placed around her neck. The ruby that was all she had left of Cagney, of what might have been. She pulled back the silky collar of her blouse to touch the necklace, which lately she'd found herself wearing more and more, even when no eye could see it.

She'd known it was most likely stolen, that the vulnerable boy she'd adored had been involved in something illegal. If only she'd had the strength to help him then, to change him. But didn't every girl in the throes of love think she could do that? If only she had kept him away from the lighthouse that fateful night. But he was on a downward spiral hanging out with those other troublemakers. She'd feared what might happen to him. Auntie Beth had forbidden her to see him. Maybe if she had obeyed her, but one does not change history.

She could still feel Auntie Beth's strong arms encircling her when years later she comforted her. "He's surely gone, Amy," she had said firmly. "Don't torture yourself anymore." Later she had learned that the ring of thieves he'd been involved with had been broken up, though the cash and jewels had not been recovered. No doubt the ruby necklace was stolen too; she should have turned it in after that awful night. But it was her wedding gift. Why this compulsion in recent weeks to wear it almost constantly— like some kind of hair shirt with which the ancient martyrs tortured themselves?

She remembered the stricken look on her aunt's face. "I don't want your name connected with any of it. No one needs to know you were anywhere near the keeper's shack and that you were eloping." And so she'd been whisked away that very night, taken home to her mother before she'd revealed the crimson necklace hidden beneath her shirt.

Amy knew in the logical part of her that Cagney was most certainly dead. Had she seen him fall? Or pushed? It had been so dark, so terrible. The brutal fight. . .and then the silence. Had she fainted? When the man turned around, scanned the group of trees where she was hiding, she'd seen his eyes: menacing, gleaming with an eerie yellow light. And still there were nights when she saw them again and again in tormenting dreams. Had he murdered Cagney?

After she turned eighteen, she had returned a few times to spend a week or two at her aunt's cottage. They picnicked and swam on the beach or sat under shady trees near the cottage with their needlework projects. Amy remained a novice crocheter, but her Auntie Beth was a wizard with a needle. Crocheting, knitting, embroidery, tapestry: she knew the intricacies of them all. And so they passed the time together but never spoke of that terrible summer. They didn't mention Cagney or the marriage that was not to be. But she could not forget. She could not forget the boy or her failure to help him when he most desperately needed her.

"You have your whole life before you, Amy. I want you to stop mooning around about some no-account drifter and get on with your education, your life." She could still hear Melanie's words spoken so long ago. She could still see herself standing by Melanie's high-backed chair, her blue nightshirt stained with sweat and tears as she faced her mother.

Is that when she had ceased calling her "Mother"? Auntie Beth was more mother to her than Melanie had ever been. After that terrible summer, she had called or phoned her aunt whenever her mother wasn't around to forbid it.

And now she often wasn't around. To be fair, Amy conceded in the quietness of her cubicle at Melanie's design company, her CEO mother had to travel frequently, and she made sure her daughter had the best of everything. The best private schools, investments for the future, connections to powerful friends. But it couldn't make up for the emptiness she felt at the center of herself. If only her mother could understand that she had loved Cagney. He wasn't just some passing fancy. She had been young, but she mourned him yet—and mourned her cowardice in his moment of darkest need.

When, stunned and broken, Amy had been brought home that summer, her mother's anger had flared. "My sister should never have allowed this to happen. She should have known better!" Stormy blue eyes narrowed in the smooth white face so carefully made up before breakfast. "Now, no more tears. Enough! You'll buckle down and study. There's plenty to do here in New York without running off to Maine."

But somewhere beneath those blue waters, the love of her life had been swallowed up. The charming old lighthouse still towered over the restless waves, its great eye seeing all, knowing all. And she had covered her face, tried to blot out the shape of the man and the fists raining down on the boy whose arms had once held her so tenderly.

"What is it?" Ev had asked quietly one evening. He had just come downstairs after putting little Peter to bed. They had planned a late dinner and a movie; Ev's sister was on her way to babysit. Amy and Ev and Peter had been in the living room of Ev's apartment, laughing over a favorite book of Peter's. It was Eric Rohmann's *My Friend Rabbit,* and Peter wanted "Miss Amy" to read to him. It was the tale in which an elephant, a rhino, a hippo, a deer, an alligator, a squirrel, a bear, and a goose all stack themselves high to help Rabbit get an airplane out of a tree.

Peter's quick, dark eyes, his luminous golden skin, and the black hair he'd inherited from his Brazilian mother sometimes startled Amy. Peter reminded her of Cagney; but the truth was, almost everything reminded her of Cagney.

"I love that story," four-year-old Peter gushed and, throwing his small arms around Amy's neck, had pleaded for her to read it again.

The feel of those warm, sticky arms had struck something deep inside her and unleashed a torrent of tears she could not stop.

Ev had said he loved her and that he hoped they might marry someday. But did she even deserve to be loved again? Suppose she failed Ev as she had failed Cagney? What if she couldn't protect Peter? She wanted to tell Ev—to tell someone! But how could she explain in words that made sense?

Afterward, she had gone back to high school, graduated, and gone on to college. She'd earned a degree in early childhood education, not fabric design as Melanie had wished. She'd at least had guts enough to defy her mother on that. Things had changed markedly between them. They'd never been close. (How could you get close to a mother who was gone more often than not?) But that summer had opened a chasm between them that Amy feared might never close.

Things had changed between Melanie and Auntie Beth, too. Like a pebble thrown into a pond, the events of that summer had caused an ever-enlarging ripple widening into a sinkhole of enormous proportions. The two did not speak, at least until it became clear that Grandma Beatrice could no longer live on her own. Then they had to talk to one another. If Mary Beth was willing to look after her in that "dreary little Rocky Point village," so be it. They consulted each other on matters of their mother's care: cold, professional conversations that gave Amy the chills. Auntie Beth had e-mailed just last week that Grandma Beatrice was ill. It wasn't just the dementia this time, that terrible disease that stole the mind and broke the heart, but something respiratory. Grandma was in a weakened condition, and at eighty-eight, the threat of pneumonia could be lethal.

"Pray for your Grandma," Auntie Beth had written.

And she had tried, but it was as though an impenetrable ceiling stopped any petitions, sent them echoing back into her consciousness. Surely God had more important things to do that listen to her pleas. Amy got up and turned away from the computer screen with its nostalgic seaside image. She walked to the window and peered unseeing into the glass. The cloudy afternoon had turned even bleaker, making her reflection the only thing she could see.

The long blond tresses of her girlhood were coaxed now into a short, tailored style that demanded little care. Her blue eyes appeared colorless and sunken beneath pale eyebrows. What had happened to that young girl of sixteen who had so much life before her. . .the young woman who last winter, at thirty-eight, had quit yet another teaching job and run back to New York? Was her life to be a series of running aways? And running to a mother who had never had time for her?

This time it had been a local tragedy that had unhinged her. When the body of a young teenager had been found in the Hudson River off Hoboken, Amy had been catapulted backward in time. She tried to ignore the news reports, to shut her eyes to the sad photograph of the boy so young and vulnerable. He too had been Hispanic, the only child of a poor immigrant. Surely she could go on with her daily routine as always. But she'd been unable to cope; in nights of broken sleep Cagney's face returned again and again. Once more she ran away.

"I am so sorry, sweetheart," Auntie Beth had said when she phoned to tell her about it.

"I'm a complete failure," she'd blurted out. "I couldn't stay. All I could think about was. . . It was just like what happened to. . ." But Cagney's name died on her trembling lips.

"You're not a failure!" her aunt had said in steely denial. Then, more quietly, "You just feel the pain of others more than most people."

She turned away from her reflection in the glass. What good did it do to feel the pain of others and not do anything to help? Not be able to help? She couldn't even help herself. She wondered if what Auntie Beth had once told Melanie were true: that Amy walked through the world as though she were naked in a briar patch.

A low rumble of thunder and a quick flash of lightning thrust her back into the moment. She had the catalog copy to finish before the day's end. She couldn't mend her sorrows, but she could at least write a few mindless adjectives about dresses and hats.

When she returned to her desk, her cell phone beeped to indicate she had a message. She took the phone out of her bottom drawer and punched in the retrieval button. She stared at the area code and number: Auntie Beth! Her fingers trembled. She'd just talked to her a couple of days before; something must have happened. Amy felt that all-too-familiar twinge in her stomach, that foreshadowing of something gone wrong.

"Auntie Beth?"

"Amy! How are you, dear?" The warm contralto voice always had the power to calm her.

"I'm okay. I. . .saw your message." Amy waited. Was there something different about her voice?

"I'm sorry to call you at work. Is it going okay?"

"Yes, yes, it's fine." She paused. "Is Grandma. . . ?"

"I'm afraid she's not doing well, Amy. She's on oxygen all the time now. It's not totally unexpected; she's been having trouble for quite some time, but. . ." Mary Beth hesitated and then said, "I think we should contact your mother, dear. Where is she? Do you have the number?"

"Oh, Auntie Beth. I was so hoping. . ." She broke off, imagining the kind face with its cloud of springy curls, the soft brown eyes. Auntie Beth had been so attentive to Grandma. But Grandma never loved Auntie Beth the way a mother should.

"Melanie's in Mexico, I think. I'll have to check with her secretary, but she may be hard to find. She's with that new artist friend of hers. . ." Amy paused.

"Let me know as soon as you can. And Amy. . .could you come?" Appeal and apology seemed to linger in her question.

It was a request she'd been dreading and longing for at the same time. She stared into the screen saver, into the dark blue ocean tumbling against rugged shale and the stately old light, white and shining in a turbulent sky. It had been two years since she'd been back to Stony Point. Two years since she'd seen her aunt, since they'd sat together on her cottage porch and watched the sun set in a golden blaze.

She put her fingers to her throat, felt the necklace beneath the delicate fabric. Had some premonition set her to wearing it again, even in the heat of summer? So the finger of fate was beckoning her back to Stony Point. Whatever was wrong with her had begun there; if anything would ever be right again, perhaps it could happen there.

"Of course," she said softly. She cleared her throat. "I'll make arrangements and come as soon as I can."

~ 16 ~

Annie rolled the Malibu back into Stony Point after a weekend jaunt to Camden with Alice, complete with an overnight stay at Abigail's Bed and Breakfast. She and Alice had promised themselves this treat. They had reveled in the shopping and dining but had faithfully worked on their needlework projects in the evening. Mary Beth would be proud of them!

Annie felt a rush of euphoria as the familiar sights came into view. The beach spilled over with sunbathers and shell seekers. Visitors in search of respite from their day-to-day cares browsed the quaint shops and restaurants. Lobster boats and pleasure crafts bobbed in the busy blue bay.

"In Texas, we'd be roasting this time of day and heading indoors to air-conditioned comfort," Annie mused. "The twins would be begging for ice cream or popsicles." She didn't miss that part of Texas, but the thought of her home and family back in the Lone Star state gave her sudden pause. LeeAnn would have whirled through household chores so the afternoon would be free to play with the twins. Maybe Herb had taken them to the water park or the Dallas Zoo.

"I guess you miss it. Or them," Alice noted presciently.

Annie sighed. The latter was true, she realized. It was strange, though, that she didn't think of her old home in

Brookfield as often these days. Without Wayne, it was merely a house anyway. A home wasn't a place; it was people. It was warmth, friendship, love; it was what she was finding right here. "I do sometimes," she said, "but being here at Stony Point has been really wonderful." Gratitude swelled inside her. "Everyone's been so good to me. And you've been wonderful, Alice."

Alice looked across at Annie. A twinkle appeared in her blue eyes, and she tossed her mane of auburn hair. "Of course I'm wonderful! You knew that back when we were kids. And don't you forget it."

Annie laughed. Alice had a special way of pulling her out of her pensive moods. "Not a storm cloud in the sky today," Annie mused. "But things can change fast around here."

"Tell me about it!" Alice said. "Like last week after our trip to the Portland Library. I forgot to close one of my kitchen windows, and I had to mop up a puddle the size of a small creek."

"It was a torrent all right," Annie affirmed. "Fast and furious. Dorian and I hardly got my windows closed in time. We were having iced tea on the porch after the gateleg table was finished, and suddenly the clouds burst open."

There was a little silence. "And how is our golden boy doing?"

Sometimes Annie thought Alice didn't really like Dorian in spite of her exclamations over his handsome face and muscular body. She often feigned jealousy, kidded her about snagging a rich, eligible bachelor.

"He's been such a help with Wally laid up, and Gram's

gateleg table is truly a work of art," Annie said. But it wasn't the table that had come to her mind so frequently since the afternoon of the storm. It was the way his muscled hands had felt on her shoulders as together they had pressed the door closed against the sweeping wind and rain. She could still feel the fleeting pressure of his lips before he left her and sprinted across the lawn.

Days went by when she didn't see him at all; then he'd suddenly appear and set to work as though he belonged there. Lately he'd started to repaint the shutters. Sometimes they had quiet talks, but she'd been careful to keep to the relative safety of the porch.

"What does he do all day?" Alice asked. "When he isn't at Grey Gables, I mean?" she added wryly.

"I don't know. He's only been around a few times." Annie paused, not wanting to share her conflicted feelings about Dorian, the almost irresistible drawing and the undeniable sense of caution.

He'd mentioned having some appointments in the area. Likely he'd combined a return visit to Stony Point with business contacts in such places as Augusta and Portland. He discussed his work briefly and, she'd noticed, usually only when she pressed him for information.

"He's still planning on hanging around until the needlework fair, isn't he?"

"Yes, far as I know. Mary Beth couldn't be happier about it. She's been spreading the news all around town. She'll hold him to it; we can be sure of that." Annie was glad to shift the focus to Mary Beth. "She's commandeered the entire Senior Center for the display and for a ministore. Kate told me they've ordered enough thread, yarn, and notions to stock China."

Alice smiled at Annie's exaggeration but gazed through the open window. "Where'd you say he went to school? University, I mean."

Annie frowned. Phoenix, Dorian had responded casually when she'd posed that question. She'd had no intention of looking it up but had found herself scrolling through institutions of higher learning in that city. She'd found no Dorian Jones registered during the years he might have attended.

"Out west," Annie said. "Phoenix, I think." She didn't want to admit that she'd been checking up on Dorian. Was she so. . .what was that Victorian term. . .besotted that she'd taken to Googling his name? Or was it that she didn't trust him? She turned onto Main Street, oddly troubled. There was also that matter of Gram humming while she worked. Well, it was a small detail. What did it matter?

"You remember I told you about my cousin who had connections with Christie's?" Alice broke in. "Well, I asked him about Dorian. You know, whether he knew him or anything." She fidgeted uncomfortably, looked out the window and then straight ahead at the dashboard. "Well, he knows just about everyone in the circuit, and he doesn't know any Dorian Jones."

Annie snatched a quick glance at her friend. "Maybe he uses a professional name in those circles," she said in as offhand a manner as she could muster. "You've lived in Maine too long, Alice," she said. "You look on all outsiders with suspicion."

"I don't!" Alice quipped without rancor. "I'm just protective of my friends. Remember, I'm wonderful! That's what you said."

"I did, and you are!" Annie said, laughing. "I'll even treat you to coffee at the Cup and Saucer before we go home and unload. What do you say?"

"You're on."

Inside the busy café, the booths were filled. Locals and summer people had sought out their favorite haunt at the height of coffee-break time, which was likely all day around the Cup and Saucer. They scanned the crowd, greeting some of the people they knew.

"Look, there's Ian and Mary Beth. Let's join them. It's either that or the counter," Alice said, charging toward the back where the two sat engrossed in conversation.

"Mind if a couple of wanderers join you?" Alice asked.

Both Ian and Mary Beth looked surprised. Alice chattered about their visit to the city, but Annie, glancing from one troubled face to the other, realized they must have interrupted a serious conversation.

Ian rose to guide Annie in next to him. Alice sat down across from them next to Mary Beth. "It sounds like you two had a good time," Ian remarked, signaling for coffee to the waitress passing in the aisle.

"It was great," Annie said. "But it's wonderful to be home." That "home" had come out quite naturally, and Annie liked the way it sounded. She thanked the young girl with the dangling charm bracelet who placed a steaming cup before her. An add-on for the summer rush, no doubt. She looked around for the familiar sight of Peggy, not to be seen.

"Where's Peggy today?" Alice asked.

Ian's rugged hands were folded on the table, but he was fidgeting restlessly. Annie saw the little muscle in his jaw working and knew something was up.

"I guess you haven't heard," Mary Beth said, frowning. "She and Wally are with Emily. At the hospital."

Alice gasped. Annie felt her stomach clench. Beautiful little Emily, Peggy and Wally's pride and joy, their world!

"Peggy took Emily to Harvard on Saturday to buy ballerina slippers," Mary Beth explained, her brown eyes dark with concern. "Jane Swenson had loaned her car to Peggy because theirs is still in the shop. They went to find the slippers Emily wanted so badly. Afterward, they left the store and. . ." Mary Beth shook her head, turned to Ian.

"They just stepped off the curb to cross the street where the car was parked when it happened," Ian finished. "A car peeled around the corner; it was too close to the curb and going like crazy. He hit Emily and then just sped away. Left her in the street."

"Oh, no!" Annie felt her stomach lurch.

"She's going to be all right," Ian added hastily. "They set her broken leg; with time and therapy it should be as good as new. . .so they say."

"Peggy and Wally are with her now. So is Reverend Wallace," Mary Beth put in. "We're sending balloons and flowers from the Hook and Needle Club, of course."

Annie, trying to absorb the dreadful information, could only imagine the trauma the couple must have endured and little Emily's shock and pain. She stared at Mary Beth and then at Ian. She saw his jaw twitch, the lines in his forehead deepen. "Have they caught him? The guy who hit her?" she asked.

Ian drew in a breath. "Yup," he said, expelling it in a long sigh. "Some kid half stoned and barely old enough to drive!" His fists came down suddenly on the table. "It's the lowlife who sold him the stuff we want to find. . .and we will."

"The police in Harvard are working on it," Mary Beth said more calmly.

Annie's heart sank. Even beautiful coastal towns like neighboring Harvard some forty miles south of Stony Point were not immune to the scourge. Evil lurked in the human heart, and it was too often poured out on innocents like Emily Carson, future prima ballerina. . .if her leg could be restored.

She had to get better. Annie pushed the dark fear down. Peggy would need help. Once Emily came home, she would offer to stay with her when her parents had to work. Thinking of Wally and Peggy's needs was a far more positive way to dispel the awful gloom she was feeling.

Annie drove Alice home and quietly helped her unload her things. Their beautiful weekend had been tainted. Annie wanted only to shut herself inside Grey Gables and enjoy its peace and comfort.

She pulled up Grey Gables' long driveway and parked the Malibu. She grabbed a few of the lighter things, planning to unload the rest later, perhaps after a cup of tea. The coffee at the Cup and Saucer had gone completely untouched.

She had stacked paint cans, tarps, and brushes at

one side of the porch in case Dorian came to paint the shutters. She'd left the ladder behind the thick lilac bushes in back, and he could get water for clean up or drinking from the outside spigot, but nothing outside the rambling house appeared to have been touched while she was gone. No doubt Dorian had been too busy with his private concerns to work on Grey Gables. Once more she recalled the brush of his lips and the heat of his hands on her shoulders. Silence hovered over Grey Gables with a heaviness she'd never noticed before.

And where was Boots? If Annie was away for more than a few hours, Boots usually awaited her return in the sunny front window.

Annie shivered, though the air was still mild. They'd stayed too long at the Cup and Saucer; it would soon be dark. She wished she'd asked Alice to stay awhile, perhaps have a late supper with her. She shifted her bundles, oddly disturbed, and turned the key in the lock.

As she stepped into the entryway, she was greeted by a loud meowing coming from upstairs. Strange. Boots seldom "spoke." And why wasn't she already at Annie's feet? Annie dropped her things at the door and followed the sound, which seemed to be coming from the attic.

"What are you doing up here?" she scolded as she pushed back the partially opened door. *That's strange*, she thought. Annie always closed the attic door. The mewing grew louder. It was coming from high up in the rafters. Astonished, Annie saw Boots way up at the peak of the attic, peering down like a miniature queen of the hill, tail switching over the ledge. "And what are you doing way up there?"

For answer, Boots uttered a few more plaintive meows but made no attempt to jump down.

"You got up there. Get yourself down. Come on." She must have leaped up from the stack of trunks along the wall. Annie maneuvered around the jumbled chaos of boxes and trunks until she could stand directly below the cat's perch. She held out her arms.

She had spent some enjoyable hours among Gram's things, but now a suffocating, dust-ridden gloom seemed to pervade the attic's dark depths. A cloying scent filled the humid airlessness—a wild, woodsy fragrance, not unpleasant but stifling in the close atmosphere. Annie felt an eerie sensation. . .as though someone else were there. She shivered. The depressing news about Emily must be what had unnerved her.

"We are not exploring today," she said sternly. But Boots took a few neat balancing steps and resumed her perch. Annie laughed, but the sound of her own voice echoed oddly in the stillness. "Haven't you heard that curiosity killed the cat?" She pulled the trunks away from the wall one at a time and restacked them so she could get up high enough to reach Boots.

"There you are!" As she reached out a hand to grab Boots, she stopped in amazement. Behind the narrow strip of flashing at the attic's peak was a shelf that ran the length of the cornice behind the rafters. Boots, quietly switching her tail, had discovered a secret hiding place.

It was too dark to see anything, and thick dust clung everywhere. What *was* that smell? In a flash she remembered. Dorian's cologne.

Her nerves a-skitter, she put Boots down and ran in search of her flashlight. She climbed back up to the dusty ledge and shone the beam across it. The shelf had depth; it was like a square column on its side and paneled in the same veneer as the upper wainscoting. She knocked on it and heard a hollow sound. Peering closer, she saw that some of the nails in the paneling were not pounded all the way in, as though some careless workman had wearied of his task. Or someone had recently dismantled it and tried to put it back together in a hurry!

She climbed down and up again, this time with a hammer, her consternation growing. Along with her confusion, she was aware of a peculiar dread. Dorian had been uncommonly interested in the attic and this decorative cornice in particular, and he must have been here recently and long enough that the smell of his cologne had been trapped inside.

She peeled back the nails with a trembling hand, lifted the top of the shelf, and stared into an empty space about two feet deep that ran the length of the apex flashing. It was coated with dust—except for a clear area about twelve by eighteen inches. Something had been there, and someone had removed it. Annie had no doubt that Dorian Jones was that someone.

~ 17 ~

The man in Room 12 of the Maplehurst Inn lay prone on the bed, the quilt and blanket not yet turned down. It was midnight but he was not asleep.

It had been quiet as a cemetery since 9 P.M. but for a light, incessant rain that droned in his ears. Beneath the bed he felt the bag like a physical presence that both exhilarated and threatened him. Only moments ago he had turned off the lamp over the desk where again he had inspected the contents of the dusty two-foot-wide duffel bag. His pulse raced. His throat was so dry it felt like his tongue might crack. He should leave now. Now before anyone discovered the bag missing. Before someone found out who he really was.

It had to be there. But until he'd carefully pulled back the dark walnut flashing and removed the paneling he couldn't be certain. Then his breath had caught, and he felt the triumph like a flame through his whole body. An unsteady smile spread across his features.

It had been so easy. The old woman had never suspected he'd hidden something there. That was more than two decades ago. Nor had the younger one imagined that the Victorian house she'd inherited contained a fortune. His fortune.

More than ten years had gone by before he could even think about returning. He'd have to wait until everyone stopped looking for him. Then when it was safe, he'd claim what was his. He'd had plenty of time to plan how he would get it. All those tedious days in the prison library. The California manslaughter charge had kept him away ten more years. (The stupid bank guard had gotten in the way.) He'd counted and recounted the treasure he'd amassed when he was little more than a kid. He'd dreamed of it like a sailor dreams of a sea siren rising out of the ocean.

Now no one remembered the tall, black-haired kid of twenty who had put into Stony Point in a fisherman's smack. He rubbed a hand over his short blond hair through which the dark roots were beginning to show again. New looks, new name, a grand show of success, and people hadn't dared question him. No one knew that two decades earlier he'd used their little village to stash a huge cache of money and jewels stolen from New England hotels.

The odd jobs he'd talked the old woman into letting him do back then had satisfied her mothering instincts and given him access to the old house. It was a perfect place to hide what the police were looking for after they began patrolling the keeper's quarters. He'd made his get-away quickly. . .after disposing of that love-sick teenager. He'd guessed that no one would care how Cage had met his death. Troublemaker that he was, they were probably glad he was gone.

He'd kept a low profile that long-ago summer. Cage had been his lookout. Things had gone along pretty well until the kid had gone moony over a girl and brought her to the shack to make out.

He hadn't seen the old place in twenty years, at least not until he'd glimpsed it in Annie's attic on a needle-work canvas. His stomach had leaped to his throat, but he'd recovered before that pretty little fox got wise. She was pretty. But what he knew about foxes was that a man couldn't trust them. Turn your back and they became the wild vixens they were.

He had found his moment when she'd told him she would be away for two whole days. It had been easy enough to climb through the window he'd made sure was left unlocked that day. That day, when he'd finally gotten inside because of a sudden rainstorm, he'd had a look in the attic at that paneling and the flashing that concealed his treasures.

He felt his stomach clench remembering the smell of her next to him as they pressed against the door. She'd certainly been soft, pliable in his arms until she suddenly went all rigid and leaped away. He unknotted his hands and reached his right one under the bed, feeling for the reassuring presence of the duffel bag. Beautiful things had endurance; people would flick you off without a second thought.

Once she had left for Camden, he had time to carefully locate his prize with only the watchful eyes of a nosy cat to worry about.

From the moment he returned to Stony Point he'd worked his charms on the widow, fielding personal questions that might give him away. He'd become Dorian Jones, respected gemologist, purveyor of all things antique. He'd fooled the whole town, since everyone believed anything Ms. Annie Dawson said. Lonely women could so easily be taken in, especially if they thought they were needed. Yes, he'd played it just right with her. . .softened her, played up to her. . .but carefully. She wasn't the kind who could be pushed around. And lately she'd seemed a bit cooler. Maybe she was turning on him like they all did. The clever foxes.

He had to get out of town. But not yet. There was one more delivery coming tomorrow. Supplying drugs to the street dealers had kept him in cash. Now with his cache he could pull out of the drug business.

He'd counted on that dumb fisherman to help him, but money hadn't been enough to buy his trust. He'd smelled a rat after only one job.

Let it go, he thought. Pretend it doesn't matter if stupid Wally helped him or not. And Wally wouldn't talk about it; he wouldn't risk that sweet little wife of his and the kid. But it could have been a perfect setup. No one would suspect the stuff was coming in by boat and that he was peddling to his contacts up and down the coast. Oh well, he'd have to collect this last one himself. Then he'd get out of Stony Point. Get out before people like that nosy mayor asked any more questions.

"Well, Mr. Jones. . .Dorian, isn't it?" The man had interrupted his breakfast in the Maplehurst dining room early yesterday morning. "Are you enjoying your vacation?" Sharp eyes did not match the wide smile he offered. He was nobody's fool, and he had a pretty big reputation around town.

He'd said all the right words, but the rough hand extended to him had been cold. Given time, Mr. Mayor might connect him to his past. Though he was no longer under the scrutiny of West Coast parole officers, his criminal past could catch up with him. No, he wouldn't think about that now.

The beautiful jeweled pieces glittered in his mind's eye. He'd remembered each one. . .the way they felt in his fingers. The diamond ring with its rose-cut center stone, accented with diamond pavé. . .nearly five karats, he'd judged. The brooch with baroque South Sea pearls, diamonds and turquoise, set in white gold, the multicolor bracelet with thirty-six sapphires. They were worth far more than the cash stacked in hundreds at the bottom of the bag. Twenty thousand bucks. A nice little bundle. But the jewels. He could almost taste them. He knotted his hands once again, rubbed them together to stop their trembling.

One piece was missing. A ruby necklace set in white gold with four Princess diamonds on each side of the center stone. It had probably gone down into the ocean with the kid. Unless he had given it to that girl. . .Amy, yeah, that was her name; some relative of that yarn lady Annie Dawson was so fond of. He'd looked for her the first day he'd arrived in town. Even seen her photo on the mantel in the yarn lady's cottage. He didn't know where she lived, but he would find her. Get that ruby necklace.

Only one more day! He'd pick up one last shipment delivered in the lobster pot, and this time maybe he'd keep the pot. Tourists always wanted one to take home as a souvenir. He felt a smile stretch across his face.

Fondling the handle of the duffel bag just beneath the bed skirt, he slept.

~ 18 ~

Mary Beth had lain awake until the first weak rays of dawn crept under her window, her mind a mix of conscious thought and absurd dream. So when her cell phone buzzed after she'd coaxed herself to sleep again, she'd known before answering that her mother, the elegant Beatrice Bennington Brock, was gone.

"My Mary. . .you always were a good girl"—the tender words Mary Beth had repeated to herself so many times since they first dropped from her mother's lips. Quick tears spilled over. "Oh, Mother."

She'd dreaded calling her sister, assuming she could find her. She'd left a message at her hotel in Cozumel. Trust Melanie to be unavailable, to be vacationing off the eastern coast of Mexico's Yucatan Peninsula when her mother was dying. She would never get to say good-bye.

Before getting out of bed, she called Amy. "Oh, Auntie Beth, I had so hoped. . ." Amy's soft, wistful voice echoed in her mind. Her niece was back in New York, a bird with a broken wing returning to the feathered nest. It would not be easy for her to say good-bye to her grandmother. Returning to Stony Point would be harder yet, especially with reports of Cagney Torrez's fate buzzing in the air. Annie's photos. Oh, Amy! Mary Beth had so hoped that by this time her niece would be able to lay her troubled past to rest. Instead, it could all be stirred up when she came to town to bid her grandmother farewell.

Mary Beth climbed out from between the covers, feeling as tired as when she'd gone to bed. If she could only undo that fateful night of two decades earlier. . .

She had been up, pacing the living room of her cottage, waiting, when the door had flown open. Amy stood ghostly pale in the black night, her sixteen-year-old face smeared with tears. Her yellow jacket hung off her thin shoulders, revealing a garish red necklace and rumpled blouse.

Mary Beth had been dumbfounded, tongue-tied.

She had been ready to demand an explanation of why the girl had sneaked out in the middle of the night. Had she been with that gang that hung out around Butler's Lighthouse? Frequent fights had occurred there that summer, and the police had been called. There'd been a lot of trouble in Stony Point that year, and Cagney Torrez was usually in the middle of it. As Amy's aunt, she was responsible for her. What had possessed Amy?

But Amy was bending over, keening like a lost soul, her hair wet and blown, pine needles trapped in its tangled tresses. Panting for breath, she fell into her aunt's arms, and Mary Beth knew something terrible had happened.

Amy admitted that she and Cagney had planned to run away together and get married. But there had been a fight. Beside herself with grief, Amy raved about someone hitting Cagney. No doubt there had been several of the teen gang there on the rocks getting into who knew what. Cagney had screamed at her to run away, to hide in the woods, and he had disappeared.

Mary Beth had gone into swift action. She had to get Amy out of there before she could be tied to whatever had gone on that night. Before anyone in the village learned that her niece had been at the keeper's cottage. Later it had been raided as police looked for stolen goods. There'd been an awful scandal. Police had swarmed the village, looking for anyone who had been involved.

Mary Beth gripped the edge of her dresser. Yes, she'd had to act fast, but she would never have packed Amy into the SUV and taken her home to her mother if she had known all that would transpire and how badly Amy would react to the loss of Cagney Torrez.

She'd only recently opened her shop. A Stitch in Time embodied her dream. She had longed for a place where people would take her to their hearts. Stony Point's citizens had done just that. They'd even bought hooks and needles and yarn they had no need for just to help her get started. If they knew Amy had been at the lighthouse that night, what would they do? And what might happen to the troubled girl whose only crime had been loving and needing to be loved?

Mary Beth felt her heart drop like a stone as she thought about it. She shouldn't have kept silent. She thought she had been protecting Amy, but the girl had never truly recovered, and justice had never been done for a troubled young boy.

"I'm all right, Auntie Beth," Amy had said much later when at eighteen she'd come back to Stony Point over Melanie's strong objections.

But Amy had not been all right. She'd gone on to finish high school, then college, and become a teacher, but she never stayed long in one place. Nor had she married. Surely she wasn't holding out because of a summer romance with a sixteen-year-old rogue.

"He's gone, Amy," she had told her. "You need to go on with your life. Be happy!" She'd wrapped her arms around the girl she'd loved since the moment she'd held her as a baby. Why hadn't she shown her the news item about Cagney's body being found in the bay? She'd been pretty sure Amy knew Cagney was dead; the girl never asked about him. They had tacitly agreed to blot out everything from that long-ago night, to pretend it never happened.

That had been a mistake too, Mary Beth thought hours later as she headed toward A Stitch in Time. She clutched the steering wheel until her knuckles whitened. If only one could go back in time. But time waited for no one.

It was Tuesday, and the club members would be arriving. Amy was on her way from New York; she'd be at the Portland Airport that afternoon. She'd taken the news pretty well. Her grandmother was dead; there would be no saying good-bye. Could she be kept from hearing about her long-ago lover? Perhaps. But what would protect her from the memories that were swallowing her happiness?

Kate had opened the shop for her so that she could begin to do what must be done when death comes. Much more needed her attention, but Mary Beth yearned for the company of her friends, if only for a little while.

From the look on their faces as she entered the room, it was clear that the dread news was known. Gwen came hurrying over, her face a study in sympathy. "I brought you one of my caramel pecan rolls. Fresh from the oven!"

Soon they were all crowding around her. "We're so sorry, Mary Beth."

"You want some cream for your coffee?"

"Here's a napkin. One of our rose blossom specials."

"Sit here; you must be tired."

Stella Brickson, her dear old friend, drew up beside her, effectively scattering the others by some inscrutable expression on her face. She took Mary Beth's arm and drew her to a chair. She sat down beside her, keeping her arm firmly tucked in her own, and the compassion in her watery blue eyes brought a sweet ache to Mary Beth's heart.

She basked in their compassionate expressions, let them seep into her weary soul. And she, the strong, always-in-control leader of the pack, had to shut her eyes against quick tears. What would she do without her Hook and Needle friends?

Their patterns, hooks and needles, and yarns were spread out before them. Annie noticed a mistake and had to rip out twelve rows. Mary Beth helped her solve the knotty problem and praised her willingness to rework the rows. Committees gave their progress reports on the fair. Someone began circulating yet another get-well card for Emily in the shape of a two-foot ballerina with a pink tutu and tiara. Mary Beth listened to their conversation, wishing she could put off what lay on the immediate horizon of her life.

"Peggy's at the hospital today," Alice said, "but she sends her love. She absolutely adored the balloon bouquet, especially the elephant in the tutu. Peggy says Emily will be able to go home soon."

"Thank God," Annie said. "I've been praying. . ." She broke off, reddened, as though she hadn't meant to speak out loud.

Mary Beth smiled. Annie had become a good friend. Mary Beth couldn't help but like her. What was it about her that made such a difference in the short while she'd been in Stony Point? Everyone depended on her. If anyone had a problem, she was right there to offer help. She had no doubt that Annie Dawson prayed every day for little Emily. She'd been such a support to Wally and Peggy too. Maybe that's what she admired most in Annie—a staunch faith that believed the best about everyone, a hope that looked for the good in every situation.

Mary Beth had been hard pressed to find a silver lining in anything that was going on in her life recently. But yes, there was one thing. The tender acknowledgment from her mother: "You always were a good girl, my Mary." The words lingered like an unexpected light in the darkness; she would hold on to them forever.

She'd planned to leave for the airport as soon as the needlework club broke up, but she really couldn't take the time to leave just now. There were arrangements to be made with Reverend Wallace and the weight of duties attached to death. What should she do? She needed Kate to handle things at the shop, which continued to do a fast-paced business. Ian was in Harvard, conferring with officials over Emily's hit and run.

Could she ask Annie to go in her place? She had no doubt that her new friend would gladly do whatever she asked. But Amy was fragile. She'd be especially vulnerable now. Her grandmother had died, ironically in Stony Point, where life had changed for Amy so long ago. Mary Beth closed her eyes, pressed her fingertips to her temples. Yes, she would ask Annie, but she had to prepare her.

The women were busy with their projects, heads bent to their work. But when Mary Beth sought Annie's face, she found those remarkable green eyes intent on her. Mary Beth got up and gestured for Annie to follow.

"I wonder if I could ask a favor," she began when they had moved away from the others.

"Of course. What can I do?"

They stood in the doorway of the back room, their voices hushed. "My niece is coming from New York. I intended to pick her up at the airport, but there's so much to do here now that Mother. . ." Mary Beth paused, unable to complete the sentence. "Ian is out of town and I need Kate in the shop. . ."

What was that look on Annie's face? Hesitation? Was there some reason she didn't want to help her? "But if you can't. . ."

"No, no. It isn't that," Annie said quickly, pressing her arm gently in protest. It's just that. . ."

Dark shadows circled Annie's eyes that Mary Beth hadn't seen before. Perhaps she hadn't slept well. In fact, she didn't look well at all. "I know it's a terrible imposition."

"It's no imposition. There's just something I had planned to do. . ." She paused, looked away with troubled eyes. "But it can wait. This is far more important." Annie's face suddenly brightened. "Please don't give it another thought. I'll be glad to go."

"I—I'll call her, tell her to meet you at the US Airways baggage claim. She's arriving on flight 3839 out of LaGuardia. Her name is Amy Martinelli. She's in her late thirties, blond, about your height, very slim, and. . ." Mary Beth paused. She pulled her wallet from the pocket of her navy Dockers. "This is Amy a few years ago, but I don't think she's changed much."

"She's lovely," Annie said. "I'm sure I'll recognize her."

"I know this is a lot to ask, but would you mind keeping her with you until I call for her at Grey Gables? I don't want her to see her grandmother until I've completed arrangements for the. . .you know. . .all that has to be done before. . ." But Mary Beth couldn't bring herself to say words like "coffin" or "body" or "burial." It would have been better if Amy had waited a day or so to come, but she had booked a flight as soon as she heard.

"Of course. Please don't worry."

"Annie. . ." She put a restraining hand on Annie's arm. "I need to tell you about Amy. She's. . .she's rather fragile. She had a bad experience in her last teaching job. And things happened here in Stony Point a long time ago that make it hard for her to come back." Mary Beth stammered. None of this would make any sense. "She. . .well, just to let you know, she'll no doubt take this hard."

"I understand," Annie said softly, eyes warm with concern. "I'll take good care of her."

But of course Annie didn't understand. How could she? Mary Beth cleared her throat and prepared to rejoin her friends. She looked from one to the other, as though to gather strength from their faces. Who could say how Amy would react if Annie should mention the fate of a young boy named Cagney Torrez?

~ 19 ~

*M*y slippers, Daddy! Can I have them right here by me?" Emily held out her arms, her eyes intent on the satiny pink ballet shoes spilling from a box by her bed. At home once more and tucked in her own bed, Emily had begged for a story. She wanted Wally to tell the one about the lost dancing shoes. He'd told it with a big flourish at the end, and then he'd hugged her and tickled her very carefully so as not to bump the ungainly cast on her leg.

On the other side of the bed, Peggy laughed and tucked the slippers into the crook of Emily's left arm. Madeline was clutched tightly at her right side. Wally smoothed the covers over them both. "Go to sleep now; I don't want to hear a peep outta ya. Got it?" he said with mock serious- ness. Peggy switched on the little praying lamb nightlight and took Wally's arm. They left the room, closing the door softly behind them.

In the living room they dropped quietly down on the sofa, their arms still hooked together. "She's home," Peggy said, eyes shining with quick tears. "I was so worried. But she's going to be all right. I'd never have forgiven myself if she'd. . ." Peggy broke off and a second later added, "I should have been watching more closely. I never saw. . ."

"Come on, honey. It wasn't your fault." Wally put an arm around her shoulder, drew her in close. "It was that kid so high he didn't know what he was doing!" He set his jaw, felt his stomach clench with anger. He loosened his grip on Peggy's shoulder when she winced. He'd been holding her too tightly. He'd been so keyed up for days, and thinking about the accident and how it happened had been driving him crazy.

He had taken Peggy back to Harvard to identify the teen—a seventeen-year-old—who'd careened too close to the curb and hit Emily. She couldn't identify him for certain. It had all happened so quickly; Peggy wasn't about to blame someone if she wasn't sure. In the end it didn't matter, because the kid admitted it. He'd been partying with friends; he hadn't meant to hit the girl, and seemed genuinely sorry. Sorrier still when his parents came to get him.

"Where do these kids get this stuff?" Peggy cried. "And he wasn't a street hood from some ghetto or something; he seemed like a nice kid!"

And that was precisely the question that was eating at Wally. Where did he get it? The police had questioned the boy about his supplier but his answers had been vague. He had no clue, said he was just some big guy he'd never seen before. A fancy dresser who always wore dark glasses. That was all Wally heard of the interrogation; he and Peggy were told they should go. But every nerve in Wally's body was suddenly on edge. Was it possible?

Something in his gut told him the day he'd delivered the package that whatever Dorian Jones was up to, it wasn't legal. He hadn't bought his story about the insurance company and a valuable antique transaction that had to be completely confidential. Could it have been drugs? Judging by the size of the package and its negligible weight, it could have been. Had the stuff that caused Emily's injury actually passed through his hands? Had he unwittingly brought about the accident that might have killed his own daughter?

Until now he hadn't admitted even to himself that there was reason to be suspicious. What did he know? Everyone talked about Dorian Jones, the big shot from New York who was sweet on Annie Dawson, the expert who would help bring in big bucks for the needlework fair. But what if he wasn't what he claimed to be? Big guy, fancy dresser. What if. . .?

He stifled the nagging possibility; it was just so crazy. The guy was a respected businessman. And big fancy dressers had to be a dime a dozen. Besides, Annie wouldn't have anything to do with someone who smuggled drugs. Unless of course she'd been fooled too, along with everyone else in town!

Wally pulled away, got up so abruptly that Peggy nearly fell over on the couch. "I'm going for a walk," he said, not trusting himself to look at her. His heart was hammering in his chest. He had to get out of there. He had to think.

"What's the matter?" She scrambled up after him. "What's wrong?"

"Nothing. I just need some air." He grabbed his jacket and left the house, feeling Peggy's wide blue eyes on him.

The night was clear and cool with only a fingernail moon behind the trees and a freckling of stars in the cobalt heavens. As he walked, he played the events of the past few days over and over in his mind: meeting Dorian on the beach, the friendly conversation, the request for a favor.

"Annie said you were a good man. Annie said you could be trusted."

Wally had told himself it was all quite normal, that it was nothing out of the ordinary. And he and Peggy desperately needed the money. But two hundred dollars to receive a package and deliver it in secret after dark?

Todd Butler had asked him just last week to keep an eye out for anything funny going on around the harbor.

"What do you mean funny?" Wally had asked.

"Ian says there's been a rise in drug activity along the coast in recent weeks. Someone may be running the stuff out of Portland."

"So, Wally Carson, do you need a two-by-four to fall on your head?" he muttered under his breath. The more he thought about it, the sicker he felt. If he went to the authorities and it turned out the package really was illegal drugs, he could face big trouble for his part in it. What would Peggy say? She might never forgive him. How could he stand that?

If the package contained legitimate antique jewelry, he'd have egg on his face big time, and everyone would be sure he was the biggest fool ever. As for Annie, she'd be really hurt. Sweet Annie who'd done so much for him and his family. But if Dorian was the sleaze bag his gut told him he was. . .and he said nothing, what might happen to her?

And who else might suffer? Maybe another child caught in the crossfire might not be as lucky as Emily. Oh, what a mess he'd gotten himself into this time!

Wally leaned heavily against the thick bark of a sugar maple and looked up at the vast unanswering sky. When he'd survived the car wreck, Reverend Wallace had told him, "The good Lord's not finished with you. He's got a plan for your life." Now the words came back to his troubled mind. If there really was a plan, he'd screwed it up royally. But he wasn't in a hurry to mess it up any more than he already had.

When it came right down to it, there was only one thing he could do that made any sense. He felt the bulge of his cell phone and lifted it out. With one more glance into the winking stars, he punched in Ian's number.

~ 20 ~

At the pilot's announcement, Amy clasped the seat belt over her lap. The brief flight from LaGuardia to Portland was nearly over. They would be on the ground soon. Over the miles, she'd given herself a good talking to and had determined to act like the mature woman she was instead of a weak, whimpering child. Meeting a stranger might help. In Mary Beth's embrace she might completely crumble. She smoothed the wrinkles from her short gray skirt and pulled out her compact mirror with unsteady fingers.

She moistened her lips and frowned at dark shadows beneath the wide blue eyes looking back at her. She raked a hand through blond curls that had been especially stubborn that morning. Her gaze stopped at her throat, lingered on the beautiful ruby with four diamonds glistening on each side of the crimson jewel.

It was fitting to wear it today, she'd decided as she dressed carefully that morning. Her soft gray suit, cut low in the bodice, provided a perfect setting for the necklace. Cagney's necklace. She lifted her chin in a defiant gesture.

She had run so long from memories, from what had happened and from what she had lost. Could she face it head on once and for all?

"I'll be here when you get back," Ev Graber had said

and stroked her cheek, his brown eyes soft with concern. "Call me, okay?" Then he'd smiled a little sadly and taken Peter's hand. They'd walked away, left her to find her gate and head for Stony Point by way of Portland.

How long would Ev's patience last? Many times she'd wanted to tell him about what had happened that long ago summer and how it had affected her ability to relate to a man. He deserved someone who could share his life and be a good mother to his son. Would it ever be possible? Could she put it all behind her and move on?

"Smile, Amy Lynn, and put your shoulders back," Grandma would say when she caught her in a low mood. "You're a Brock, and we Brocks don't give in."

And now Grandma was gone. The elegant, demanding woman she had loved in spite of all her prickles. Melanie would be getting her messages and soon wend her way to Stony Point too. Like threads from a torn and battered garment, their little family would be gathered together. . . willing or not. Only time could tell if a hand could weave the ragged pieces together again.

"I'm so sorry I can't meet you in Portland," Auntie Beth had said. "There are so many details to attend to; I can't get away just now. But Annie is coming. You remember, I've told you about her. She's a good friend." Her aunt's confident voice comforted her as it had so frequently through the years.

She'd heard a lot about how Annie Dawson had come to Grey Gables where Elizabeth Holden had lived, how she'd joined the Hook and Needle Club. Amy wondered if Annie was like Mrs. Holden, a quiet, smiling woman who had found time for everyone—especially the teen-agers whom most people viewed with bewilderment or disdain. Mrs. Holden was the surrogate grandmother for lonely kids whose families had little time for them. When summer jobs were hard to come by, she often found work for them at her house. What did she call it? Grey Gables. Yes, that was it.

Mrs. Holden had been kind to Cagney, tried to help him fit in. But he'd stayed away from the other kids, didn't trust them. And they kept their distance from him and his father. She supposed he was a better gardener than a father. She'd been warned to avoid Cage Torrez, who kept company with a pretty rough crowd. And there was one man Cagney was especially afraid of. A tall man with thick black hair and heavy brows.

"Deck don't want nobody knowing about this shack; he keeps stuff here. He'd kill me if he knew I brought you here." Amy suddenly recalled that name. Cage had called him Deck. Short for Decker? Whoever or whatever he was, Cage had both idolized and feared him.

She shut her eyes against the memory of the man she had seen pummeling Cagney. She recalled a glint of silver as huge fists crashed down on his head. Had that been a gun in his hand? She shuddered, remembering how she had swooned and pressed her hands over her face. She had opened her eyes, peered out from the thick cover of trees, and tried to make out the scene on the huge, craggy rocks. Cagney was gone.

Only that awful man with the frightening eyes remained, searching the black night for anyone who might have witnessed the fight. There was menace in their amber gleam and more: the promise that he would not forget. He would find her. Someday he would find her.

~ 21 ~

Annie sat on a low plastic chair in sight of the luggage carousel and watched the arrival monitor. Mary Beth's niece would soon be among the passengers coming down the long corridor to claim their baggage.

She suppressed a yawn and straightened in the slippery chair. Her eyes felt grainy and sore. She'd finally fallen asleep just before daybreak after struggling with what to do. Now it was nearly seven o'clock in the evening and she'd not yet come to a decision.

When she had discovered the hidden shelf in the attic and become aware that something was recently disturbed there, she'd been shocked and bewildered. Her mind had gone immediately to Dorian, not only because the aroma of his cologne had been so strong, but also because he had been inordinately curious about Grey Gables. Especially the attic. He had taken something from Gram's house. Correction: *her* house!

But what? And why? He had been so attentive, so flattering. She'd begun to think she could care for someone again. Wayne had left a vacuum no one would ever really fill, but she had been drawn to Dorian Jones. (Was that who he really was?) He had made her believe she was still desirable. But it had all been a sham. How could she have been so foolish?

She had wanted to storm into town, bang on his door at the posh Maplehurst Inn, and demand that he return whatever it was he had taken! Or go to the police and report a robbery. But what had he stolen? She couldn't name it, and nothing else had been disturbed. Nothing broken. . .except her heart. And her pride.

Better to sleep on it, wait until morning. First thing after breakfast she'd talk to Alice, who had been suspicious of Dorian almost from the start. She drew in her breath and let it go in a long sigh. She'd been fooled by his success, his magnetic good looks, by a certain need in him that called for help. There had been clues that he wasn't who he claimed to be. She'd been too blind to see them.

When she saw him again, would he pretend that nothing had happened? Would he come around, feign continued interest in her? And what about his promise to be auctioneer at the needlework fair? Or had he already left Stony Point, his mission accomplished? Then she would have to face the disappointment and bewilderment of the whole club, and especially Mary Beth.

"Can we have lunch tomorrow, Alice? Right after the Hook and Needle meeting?" She'd struggled to keep her voice even. "There's something very important I need to talk to you about."

But before she had a chance to talk to Alice, she'd gotten the news. Mrs. Brock was dead, and Mary Beth needed someone to pick up her niece at the airport.

Annie had little doubt of the identity of the blond woman now approaching the luggage carousel, deep blue eyes scanning the area. She was elegant in a soft gray suit and burgundy heels. A stunning necklace circled her neck. Red like her shoes and lipstick.

"Amy Martinelli?" Annie held out a hand.

The voice was soft and slightly lyric. "Are you Annie Dawson?"

"That's me. I'm very happy to meet you but so sorry about your grandmother. I lost mine not long ago; I know how hard it is."

Amy retrieved a small burgundy bag from the conveyor belt, and the tension in her face lessened a little. She turned to Annie with a smile. "Thank you for coming all the way here. I'm sorry the plane was so late." Annie took Amy's arm and guided her to the exit.

Settled in her Malibu and threading through highway traffic, Annie tried to put her passenger at ease. At first Amy remained quiet. Her gaze was fixed on the landscape, but gradually she began to return casual conversation. She spoke about teaching, about New York, and her current hiatus to write ads for her mother's fashion line. But as the miles passed, she became uneasy. The nearer they came to Stony Point, the more agitated Amy seemed to become. She fidgeted, her hands frequently reaching up to clutch the lovely jewel at her neck.

"She's very vulnerable right now. Something happened here years ago that makes it difficult for her to come back to Stony Point." Mary Beth's cryptic warning had contained a plea for gentleness. Annie had no right to probe, nor did she want to insinuate herself now; but she could see that Amy was obviously troubled. What could have happened that caused such ongoing distress?

Presently Annie said, quite casually, "That's a beautiful necklace you're wearing. I don't think I've ever seen one quite like it."

Amy continued to peer out the window where a drizzling rain had intensified. She said nothing at first; perhaps she hadn't even heard. Then she turned suddenly to look directly at Annie's profile. "Thank you. I got it right here in Stony Point. It was a gift from. . ." Her words died away; then as though she'd come to some decision, she spoke again quite abruptly. "It was given to me by an old boyfriend of mine. I was quite young, sweet sixteen, and he was incredibly handsome. We spent hours climbing on those huge rocks over there." She pointed toward the coast where waning rosy light outlined the great craggy shoreline. "And sometimes we'd go looking for red chiton and periwinkle shells along the beach." She rambled in a continuing stream as though some fountain had been opened to release a pent-up flood.

"He was a summer visitor like me. My Auntie Beth. . . sorry, I can never call her anything else. . .she's always been very special, and we used to spend a lot of time together when she lived in New York. So when she moved to Stony Point and I was a teenager. . .she asked me to come and spend the summer. That's where we met and. . ."

And then the river of words dried up. Startled, Annie searched for a suitable comment. "I see," she began but fell silent when she saw Amy cross her arms over her chest and bend forward. A strangled sob issued from her lips. She began to rock a little, forward and back, the necklace swinging at her throat.

Annie reached into her side pocket, withdrew a tissue, and held it out to her distressed passenger. Annie could feel the wind tugging them in unison with Amy's rocking. She slowed down almost to a crawl as rain pelted the roof of the car. When they drove into the town limits of Stony Point, she drew up along a curb and stopped. "Amy, I'm so sorry. This is such an emotional time for you. You must love your grandmother very much. It's hard when someone we care about dies. But your Grandma was so sick. She. . ."

"No. No. No," Amy said. Each syllable was choreographed to match the rocking rhythm, which abruptly stopped. Annie waited while Amy drew in a noisy breath and released it in a shuddering stream. "This isn't about my grandmother. This is about. . ." She paused. "This is about my life, and the mess I'm making of it."

Annie reached over to touch Amy's arm. "Amy, I'm sure you haven't had any supper. I know a quiet little restaurant just across the street over there. Maplehurst Inn. We could have a cup of tea, maybe a sandwich. You must be hungry. And we could talk."

Amy said nothing but nodded her head, slowly at first and then more eagerly. She sniffed, blew her nose.

The possibility of meeting Dorian flashed into Annie's mind but was quickly squelched. Amy's need was more important. They ducked inside quickly without aid of umbrellas.

When they were seated, Annie ordered hot tea for each of them and two plain turkey sandwiches. Amy had pulled herself together and was sitting demurely, hands in her lap, an unreadable expression on her pale face. Surprisingly, she began to speak in soft but measured tones, as though she'd made a decision from which there was no turning back.

"The boy I was telling you about. . .who gave me this necklace. . .we. . .um. . ." She hesitated, but only briefly. "We were lovers. We planned to run away, because my mother would never have agreed to our marriage. Nor would my Auntie Beth." She looked down at her hands briefly and then continued. "Auntie Beth had warned me about going out with him, because he'd been in a lot of trouble. I didn't want to believe it; I couldn't. I was so. . .well, I loved him. Really loved him. I never saw Cagney again after that night when he. . ."

Annie coughed. She'd swallowed too fast. The tea cup nearly fell from her hand. Had she heard correctly? Cagney? Cagney Torrez?

"I'm sorry," Amy said, dropping her eyes to her lap. "I know how this must sound. I just ran away when he was in trouble. I never tried to find him—if he's even still. . . alive! I've tried to go on with my life, to make up for what I did, but I can't seem to get over it. I think about what might have happened to him all the time. I haven't even been able to talk about it. I mean, really talk about it to anyone until now."

Annie tried to find her voice. She set the cup down carefully, touched a napkin to her lips. Then very gently, she reached across the table to grasp Amy's hands. "Everyone makes mistakes. But we can learn from what has happened and with God's help overcome them." She paused to squeeze the trembling hands lightly. "I'm honored that you shared this with me."

Tears were falling down Amy's cheeks, but she was listening quietly.

"Reverend Wallace once reminded me that every saint has a past and every sinner has a future. That's what grace is all about. And if God is willing to forgive, and I know he is, then we can't do less than forgive ourselves."

They sat in silence for several moments, the tea long since cooled before them. Finally Amy said, "I wish I'd met you long ago, Annie."

"Well," Annie said gently. "We're friends now. And Stony Pointers have to stick together. Why don't you finish your sandwich? You've got to be starved."

Like an obedient child, Amy took a generous bite and followed it with a sip of the cold tea. Then, as though a dam had been opened, she told Annie about the trouble she had experienced growing up, her desperate loneliness, and her sadness about that long ago summer. Gradually, in the dim incandescence of the nearly empty dining room, a kind of peace hovered as they talked and shared. A lone candle flickered in the center of the white tablecloth, and Annie felt hushed, as though a holy presence lingered.

When a low exchange of voices drew their gaze, they looked up. A waiter was ushering in a customer. Dorian Jones.

There he was, tall and perfectly groomed in a silk shirt and dress slacks, a shiny buckle at his waist. He was coming directly toward them. The pungent aroma of his cologne nearly stopped her breath, and she wondered if she could speak.

"Annie. What a surprise to find you here. I was just thinking about you."

She gripped the edge of the table with one trembling hand and willed herself to stay calm. The seconds ticked by as she struggled to react; then she became aware that he was not looking at her at all. His eyes were riveted on Amy and her lovely necklace.

"Ah, but I've interrupted your dinner," he said quite casually, smoothly. "I am sorry." He paused, obviously waiting to be introduced. His face had flushed slightly, which made his eyes glitter in the candlelight—that odd shade of amber.

"Hello, Dorian," Annie said with forced control. This was not the time to confront him, but she would. Oh, yes, she would. She made a show of pushing back her plate, cup, and napkin. She cleared her throat. "Actually," she said, rising, "my friend and I were just leaving. Sorry we can't stay and chat." And she fairly pulled Amy by the hand and didn't stop until they were inside the Malibu.

Undoubtedly, she had been rude, and only a dolt wouldn't have noticed, but all Annie wanted to do was get them out of there. They were several yards down the road before she turned to glance at Amy, whose hand, she realized when she grabbed it was wet with perspiration. Her face was deathly pale, and her arms clasped across her chest. She fixed wide eyes on the dashboard.

"Are you all right?"

"That man," she stammered. "What, what did you call him?"

She narrowed her eyes to better see Amy's face in the dark. The girl was visibly shivering. Things had been going so well; if only he hadn't shown up and interrupted their progress. Now Amy was all upset again. "I'm so sorry to drag you out of there, but I. . .it's a personal matter. I didn't want to talk to Mr. Jones. Never mind. We'll be at my house soon. Your aunt will come for you as soon as she can."

Annie pressed hard on the accelerator, eager to get Amy inside in the comfort of her living room. The rain had chilled the summer night, leaving it bleak and disquieting. Amy, spent after releasing long-pent-up memories, continued to stare, silently, into the dashboard.

Annie pressed the Malibu to move faster. Her personal problems with Dorian would have to be sorted out, but right now Amy needed to get inside where it was warm and dry. Grey Gables loomed dark and hulking in the stormy night as they approached. Why hadn't she left a light on? And as though Amy's mood were contagious, Annie felt herself shivering with some unnamed dread.

~ 2 2 ~

nnie parked the car close to the house. Rain continued to fall, though the wind had lessened, leaving in its
wake a stunned and silent landscape. "Come on. Just
leave your things in the car for now."

She unlocked the door, pressed Amy inside, and led
her to the sofa where a woolen afghan lay in readiness on
the cushion. Boots leaped down, dismayed at the two rain-
soaked women who'd interrupted her nap.

"Wrap this around you," she told Amy. "I'll get a towel
and put the kettle on. You hardly touched your tea at the
restaurant."

"Annie, wait," Amy said, her eyes wide. "That man you
call Dorian. I. . .I think I know him and. . ."

Annie sat down next to her and switched on the low
lamp next to the couch. She turned to the stammering Amy,
who looked as though she'd seen a ghost. "What is it, Amy?
What's wrong?"

"He was there. . .that night. That man. . .those eyes. . ."
Her eyes darted back and forth as though she were seeing
something in the air. Then she clutched the ruby necklace
with one shivering hand.

"Amy, talk to me. Try to calm yourself, and talk to me,"
Annie said firmly.

She swallowed in an apparent effort to control her voice. "Cagney called him 'Deck.' He was the one who. . ." She shook her head violently as though to make whatever she was seeing go away.

"The one who what, Amy?"

"I didn't tell you everything about Cagney. The night he disappeared into the water, we were going to the keeper's house. Cagney worked for Deck. He was the one who hit him. He. . ." Amy's eyes filled. "Cagney tried to get up, but he kept hitting him. And then Cagney went over the cliff. I was hiding in the woods. I don't think Deck saw me, but I saw him! I saw those eyes. Oh, Annie, I could never forget those eyes."

Falteringly, Amy described how she had run back to Mary Beth's cottage and told her aunt there had been a fight at the lighthouse and that Cagney was gone. No one except Mary Beth knew that Amy had been there. Mary Beth had driven through the night to take her home to her mother in New York.

Annie listened in stunned silence. Her mind whirled with what she was hearing and what she recalled from newspaper accounts. Could Dorian have been part of that gang of hotel thieves? The stolen jewelry and cash had never been found. Was it possible that Dorian or "Deck" had hidden it in Stony Point? Maybe in the attic of a compassionate elderly woman who'd given him odd jobs to do?

"Annie, if you know him, you've got to be careful." Amy shuddered and reached out a hand imploringly. "He's dangerous. I think he. . ." She stared as though gripped by a sudden insight. ". . .I think he killed Cagney that night."

But before Annie could speak, the lamp suddenly snapped off. The hall light she'd switched on when they came in went off too, as did the porch light. Silence fell like a heavy drape and wrapped around them as Grey Gables was plunged into total darkness.

Neither spoke. Boots growled low in her throat, ears erect and tail switching. Amy gasped and clapped a hand to her mouth. Her eyes projected terror as she looked into Annie's. At the same moment they heard the distinct rattle of the front door only a few feet from where they huddled on the living room sofa.

"Don't make a sound!" Annie whispered fiercely. She grabbed Amy by the hand and fled to the kitchen. She knew it was Dorian. He was coming for. . .what? Did he know Annie had discovered what he'd done, and was he coming after her? Or was he coming for Amy? If she'd seen him that night, he might have seen her. But why wait twenty years to come after her? Unless he couldn't or didn't know how to find her?

Where could they hide? Dorian knew every nook and cranny of Grey Gables. There was no time to stop and make a phone call, and her cell phone was in her purse by the front door. "Dear God, help us," she whispered, as she pulled Amy to the back door. He would search the house first. Perhaps outside they could buy some time.

"Hello-o! Anyone home?" It was him! The smooth baritone voice feigned friendliness but a mocking undertone chilled Annie to the bone.

Boots, still growling, suddenly emitted a terrible hiss. From the kitchen Annie heard a scuffle, the sound of something breaking. The vase by the front door? Then Dorian's curse and a howl from Boots. *Run, Boots*, she pleaded silently.

She opened the back door, nodded for Amy to go through. If she could just close it quietly behind them so he didn't know they'd left the house . . . But a ferocious blast of wind tore the knob from her hand, sent the door flying outward and banging back against its frame. "Run, Amy!"

They ran blindly at first and then toward the woods that bounded Grey Gables behind the house. The wind had resumed its vehemence. It tore through the leaves of thick maples and oaks, making a keening noise like weeping. Annie kept hold of Amy's hand, pressing deeper and deeper into the woods. How far had they run? And which way were they going? She could feel the panic restricting her ability to think. "Get down. Stay absolutely still!" She pulled Amy down in a thick clump of bushes entangled with trailing vines and fallen branches of sycamore. Wide wet leaves formed a canopy over them. In the hushed stillness they waited with shallow breath and thumping hearts.

Why hadn't she been able to see what Dorian was? Why hadn't something innate within her discerned his unworthy motives? Instead she'd involved him in the needlework fair, convinced Mary Beth and everyone else that he was Mr. Wonderful. What would her new friends think of her now? Would they be eager to ship her back to Texas? Alice had seen through "Wonder Boy's" handsome veneer. And Ian had warned her to be careful. What had they seen that she had not? *Oh, Wayne, if only you.* . .She stopped herself.

Whining and self-blame were useless and stupid. *Help us, Lord!*

Suddenly she knew Dorian was near, right there in the woods with them; she could smell him, the pungent cologne mixed with sweat and rain. A sweetly insidious voice wafted through the dense wood. "Amy. . .Annie. . .Come out, come out wherever you are! Then a sing-song, cajoling tone: "Come now, you know I'm going to find you."

There was a pause. He must have stopped to listen. She imagined him looking one way and then another to detect their hiding place. She felt Amy's fingernails penetrate the skin of her arm right through her sopping shirt.

"Why are you running from me? Come on, Annie dear. You know me." He took a few more muffled steps and stopped. "All I did was recover what was mine." A low mirthless laugh followed. "I guess you discovered my little visit to your attic." His tone grew harsher with each syllable. "And here I thought I'd nailed that compartment up and left it just like it was. How clever of you."

Annie's heart was pounding so loud, she was sure he could hear it. Next to her, Amy's breath came in short, anguished gasps like someone strangling.

"You know, Annie, we might have parted friends, but now you've taken up with little Amy," the taunting voice continued. "Little Amy knows what I want; don't you, Amy?"

A half cry escaped Amy's lips, and her hand flew to her throat.

"I just want what's mine." The saccharine plea ended in a hostile outburst. "What I waited for all those stinking years."

Annie swallowed and felt her heart leap to her throat. She heard the sound of steps. He was still several yards away, but he was coming directly toward them.

"Come on, now," he crooned. "I'm not going to hurt you. Not if you'll just hand over what is mine."

Their faces were pressed together in the thick brush, so close that Annie could feel Amy's cold wet cheek. She met her terrified eyes, willed her to understand it was time to run again.

She leaped up, yanking Amy along, and ran. He was right behind them, crashing through the tangled brush and sticks. They'd gone the length of her property and doubled back twice. She judged they were now a few hundred yards from Alice's cottage, and Annie could see pale light flickering through the trees. They'd soon be out in the open space; they'd be plainly visible. There would be no place to hide. But there was nothing else to do.

As they burst into the clearing, the landscape suddenly lit up like the Fourth of July. A blast like a hundred horns blared. And then she saw them, her neighbors. They'd lined their cars up around Grey Gables in battle formation. And one of them. . .could it be? Yes, it was Ian tackling an astonished Dorian who'd burst through the trees right behind her and Amy. Wally, with his one good arm, was battering their assailant as he struggled with Ian.

Police joined the melee amid shouts and cries and the whine of sirens. Annie felt herself pulled into outstretched arms. It was Alice!

Mary Beth had Amy in a fierce embrace. Both of them were being led quickly away from the edge of the wood to the ring of watching neighbors. A flashlight-wielding Mike Malone stood near Kate Stevens, who wrapped a blanket over Annie's shoulders. From the corner of her eye, Annie could see Stella peering anxiously through the window of Jason's old Lincoln Continental.

She could only stammer her wondering gratitude to friends who had not abandoned her but had been watching over her like avenging angels. Somehow they had known how very much she needed them!

～ EPİLOGUE ～

Annie leaned back in the wicker chair across from Alice. On a low table, crystal glasses and a pitcher of lemonade sparkled in the sunshine. Alice's fragrant bread circled one of Gram's Aster Blue plates. Above them, a serene blue sky cuddled small white clouds in motherly arms and watched over an ocean as content as a sleeping child.

"On a morning like this, it's hard to believe there's anything harsh or wrong in the world anywhere," Annie said dreamily.

A week had gone by since Amy's arrival, her startling revelation, and the harrowing chase through the woods. Annie had heard the story several times: how Wally had gone to Ian about the suspicious package delivered in the moonlight. His confession had set the whole rescue in motion, but the police had already been closing in on Dorian Jones, aka Jake Decker, thanks to Ian's investigation.

Decker, recently released from a California prison, had been linked to the twenty-year-old East Coast theft of a half million dollars in cash and jewels. The police had searched his room at Maplehurst Inn and found the cache under the bed. That's when they came looking for Dorian.

"Mary Beth called me right away," said Alice. "When she came to pick up Amy at Grey Gables and found the doors wide open and no one around, she knew something was wrong. The news that you might be in trouble traveled fast," Alice said. She ran her many-ringed fingers through auburn hair and grinned. "We were all around you; Chief Edwards was even inside the woods, trailing you."

"That would have been comforting to know at the time," Annie said, rolling her eyes. "But I can't tell you how glad I was to see all of you there; I'm so grateful." She traced the slow passage of a distant boat. "You were right about him," she said, closing her eyes, but she couldn't shut out the vision of Dorian Jones.

Behind those haunting eyes and handsome face, evil lurked inside him. She believed, as Reverend Wallace said, that everyone born is prone to evil. But it can be overcome by the power of good, which also marks every individual created in the image of God. She'd looked for those stirrings of good in Dorian and longed to foster them. She sighed, realizing she had seen only what he wanted her to see. "I don't know how I could have been so taken in, so. . ."

"No one knew," Alice interrupted. "He covered his real self very well. That phony façade, those expensive clothes, and that high-toned accent. And the fact that he once worked for Betsy Holden. It's no wonder you were intrigued. That he might have known your grandmother, spent time with her, was an irresistible tie."

"I suppose," Annie said wistfully. "He hurt a lot of people, especially Amy. And Cagney."

"Mary Beth was nearly beside herself when she found out. Amy told her everything about that night; told the police, too, exactly what she saw. She remembered things she'd never really admitted to herself, let alone to anyone else. Now that Cagney's killer has been arrested, she may finally be able to put the whole thing to rest. She claims you had a lot to do with that."

Annie felt a sweeping sadness as she thought about Amy and Cagney. Parents who should have loved and guided them had failed them both. Perhaps there'd be justice for Cagney and certainly hope for Amy. Melanie was in town, having come for Beatrice Brock's funeral. After years of estrangement, they might salvage some semblance of family loyalty.

"If you hadn't pursued that mystery photo in the album, no one would have known what happened to Cagney. And a crook might have gotten away with robbery and murder." Alice paused. "You know, Dorian, or Decker, or whatever his name is, wasn't very smart. No wonder he was doing time for several bungled burglaries. You'd think he would lie low, but he wasn't content just to recover the cache he'd hidden in your attic. Oh, no. He went right on working his sideline business practically in our back yard!"

Annie frowned. "Yes, and thanks to me, Wally almost got caught up in it."

"Wally needed money. But he suspected Dorian was into something shady. It was eating him up. When he called Ian and told him about the package, it put the police one step nearer to tying Dorian to illegal activity along the coast, which had been ramping up, as well as to the hotel thefts twenty years ago. No coincidence that it was about the time he got out of prison in California and traveled east."

"I feel so bad about what happened to Emily," Annie said softly.

"When Wally learned that Emily's accident had been caused by a kid who was using illegal substances, his conscience wouldn't let him alone. Peggy told me Wally was miserable. He called Ian to confess." Alice looked meaningfully at Annie. "Dorian's out of commission. And Emily is going to be fine. So no more beating yourself up about Wonder Boy. He's going back to prison where he belongs."

While Alice bent to her intricate cross-stitch, Annie worked her crochet hook through the soft red bouclé that was becoming Joanna's sweater. They'd lost a lot of time in recent days with everything that had happened; and there was still a needlework fair in the offing. Mary Beth had insisted on going forward with their plans, persuading her sister to be the judge. *Wonders never cease*, Annie thought, and lifted a grateful heart in praise to God.

As for the auction, Ian was planning to hire a professional auctioneer. The insurance company had been so pleased to recover the stolen goods, they were considering a reward for the village of Stony Point. The town council agreed that investing in the needlework fair was worthwhile and a good business decision.

"Did I tell you Amy's going to stay for a couple weeks?" Annie said thoughtfully. "She wants to help Mary Beth design some posters for the fair. She says there's so much to catch up on in Stony Point." Annie lifted her gaze to the distant ocean, its colors shifting from gray to blue in a thousand different hues. "She wants to bring someone special to see it too, someone who makes her eyes dance. Isn't it marvelous?"

"A lot has happened since you first found that photo album," Alice said thoughtfully.

"Actually, we can blame that on Boots. She knocked it down from somewhere in the attic."

Boots, who had been sitting quite demurely in a patch of sunlight on the porch rail, got up and stretched. With a sound that was half purr and half meow, she jumped up on Annie's lap and looked expectantly into her face.

"I should have taken a cue from this clever cat," she said. "I always wondered why she disappeared whenever *he* came around."

"Cats have an innate sense about people, I guess."

"She always avoided him." Annie paused, smiled. "At least until he broke into Grey Gables that night." She recalled the fearsome howl and hissing and Dorian's curse when Boots had finally demonstrated her utter disdain and inflicted a sizable scratch across his nose. Annie stroked the silken ears. "Come to think of it," she said with sudden realization, "if Boots hadn't been carrying on that night way up in the attic, I'd never have found that secret compartment."

Boots blinked her prescient green eyes, twirled around twice, and curled herself into a ball. Annie didn't scold her for sitting on Joanna's sweater. Boots was part of Grey Gables, Gram's wonderful old house that belonged now to her. She let her eyes roam over the lush green trees and the garden resplendent with Michaelmas daisies and riotous roses. She imagined Gram bending over to cut a tall stalk of salvia or a spray of purple asters, saw her pause and lift her eyes to heaven.

Annie smiled. Had she too found a home? Not just a house but a home where friends and neighbors looked out for one another. A place where you could know that what-ever came—be it for good or ill—could be faced together.

Annie traced the flight of a lone seagull across the distant horizon. Its plaintive call echoed like the cry of a lost child seeking its home. Sunlight turned the bird's wings silver as it soared farther and farther until it reached Butler's Lighthouse and came to rest at its glistening peak.